RAMAYAN

India's Classic Story of Divine Love

By Sage Valmiki

Retold by P. R. Mitchell

iUniverse, Inc.

New York   Bloomington

Ramayan

India's Classic Story of Divine Love

iUniverse books may be ordered through booksellers or by contacting:

*iUniverse
1663 Liberty Drive
Bloomington, IN 47403
www.iuniverse.com
1-800-Authors (1-800-288-4677)*

*ISBN: 978-0-595-50763-4 (pbk)
ISBN: 978-0-595-61639-8 (ebk)*

Printed in the United States of America

iUniverse rev. date: 1/30/2009

Dedicated To
Srila A.C. Bhaktivedanta Swami Prabhupada

A great devotee of Lord Ram

ACKNOWLEDGMENTS

I WOULD LIKE TO thank Mary Linn Roby, for executing such a fantastic edit and brightening up the text, Dr George Chryssides for providing the foreword, and last, but no means least, Vishnudas, for the amazing cover painting.

Thanks to all.

The only thing necessary for the triumph of evil is for good men to do nothing.

Edmund Burke

FOREWORD

PERHAPS THE SCHOOL PUPIL who defined it as "something that is false on the outside, but true on the inside" gave one of the most apt definitions of "myth." Whether the story "really happened that way" is something that admits of different views among those who subscribe to the religion from which the story arises, but the important issue is what the story teaches.

To attempt to explain the *Ramayan's* meaning in this foreword would be inappropriate. Good narrative speaks for itself, and its point is to bring alive what might otherwise be dull abstract explanation about human behavior, devotion, divine providence, and the assurance of good triumphing over evil. Religious stories also take on new meanings and give fresh insights, the more often they are recounted by succeeding generations. The telling and retelling of a well-known story is therefore important, and in recounting once again the *Ramayan's* story in his own distinctive way, P. R. Mitchell has imbued it with a welcome freshness.

It is appropriate that Mitchell frames his narrative by demonstrating how widely the *Ramayan* has been circulated, and not merely in recent times. The *Ramayan* is more than a piece of literature, as recounted here, but has had significance for art, architecture, theatre, music and dance. Devotees of Ram, Sita, Lakshman and Hanuman have become acquainted with their faith largely through such stories. For those who are less familiar with the Hindu religious tradition, what better way is there to become acquainted with its ideas than through reading its stories? I very much hope that P. R. Mitchell's rendering of the *Ramayan* will be enjoyed by "insiders" and "outsiders" alike, as it deserves to be.

Dr. George D. Chryssides, M.A., B.D., D.Phil.

Research Fellow in Contemporary Religion
University of Birmingham, UK.

INTRODUCTION

THERE ARE MANY VERSIONS of *Ramayan* available, yet the story is not generally known in the West. This edition is aimed at the Western reader who may not be familiar with the epic, but is fond of rousing adventure.

Written many thousands of years ago by the poet Valmiki, *Ramayan* is an epic adventure encompassing all that is best in great stories, a supernatural tale of love, wisdom, separation, war, pain, morality and ultimately, justice.

Throughout the story, the hero, Ram, faces many trials that test, as a well as tax his endurance to the limits.

Valmiki's *Ramayan* is the most authoritative version of India's epic classical tale of eternal love and wisdom, centering on the Warrior Prince hero, Lord Ramachandra, and has left its mark on the consciousness of man with truths that are as germane today as they were thousands of years ago.

Valmiki was a sage known for his great austerity. One day, as he sat on the bank of the river Tamasa, pondering over a problem, Narada Muni, the celestial musician, son of Lord Brahma, appeared at his side.

Narada Muni, knowing as he did, the thoughts of all, and seeing that Valmiki was troubled, questioned him about it.

"My dear Narada," Valmiki replied. I want to know who is the most perfect, most virtuous person in all the three worlds, friend to all, upholder of truth, defender of the weak, a man who is humble, valiant, and capable of great self control in the face of sensory temptation. He is a man who refrains from criticism, a knowledgeable man who the gods fear. This I desire to know."

"I know of such a person," Narada said without hesitation. "He is a descendant from the Ishvaku line, a famed warrior prince, and is the ideal king, protector of the oppressed, and husband of Princess Sita, daughter to King Janaka of Mithila. His name is Ram."

And with that, Narada proceeded to narrate the tale of Ram to Valmiki. When he had finished, Valmiki returned to his *ashram*. On the way there, he saw two krancha birds mating in a tree. Suddenly, one fell to the ground, dead, struck by an arrow. Valmiki apprehended the hunter who fired the fateful shot, and cursed him. Later, when Valmiki related the story to his disciples, he found, that as he repeated the curse, that it sounded like a rhyme, and wondered how it had come to him so easily.

As Valmiki went about his duties, Lord Brahma, the first created living being, and *Creator demigod*, appeared, and heard him reflecting aloud on the verse he had come upon so unexpectedly.

Lord Brahma understood. "That is called a sloka," he said. "The fact that it has come to you proves that you have hidden talent. I want you to compose the poem about Lord Ram, related to you by Narada, in the same manner. You will know what is in the mind of all the characters, and therefore will write honestly, without ambiguity. When you have finished, the story of Ram and his trials will be remembered for all time, as will you, the teller of the tale."

Then Lord Brahma disappeared.

Valmiki was in awe. After regaining his composure, he sat down and proceeded to write the story of *Ramayan*, which came to him complete in the form of 24,000 verses; comprising five hundred chapters divided into six sections.

It has been predicted that the *Ramayan* story will be re-told in different times and places for millennia to come, and according to authoritative sources, was written down at least 800,000 years ago. Before that it was handed from generation to generation by word of mouth.

The hero of the story is Prince Ram, son of King Dasarath of Ayodhya, who was an incarnation of God, and every man, woman and child in India knows the story of Ram and his fight with the demons.

This version of Valmiki's *Ramayan,* with correct chronological presentation of the stories, and based on the edition from Gita Press, Gorakhpur, is an original adaptation aimed at western readers.

INVOCATION

Praise to Válmíki, bird of charming song,
Who mounts on Poesy's sublimest spray,
And sweetly sings with accent clear and strong
Ráma, aye Ráma, in his deathless lay.

Where breathes the man can listen to the strain
That flows in music from Válmíki's tongue,
Nor feel his feet the path of bliss attain
When Ráma's glory by the saint is sung?

The stream Rámáyan leaves its sacred fount
The whole wide world from sin and stain to free.
The Prince of Hermits is the parent mount,
The lordly Ráma is the darling sea.

Glory to him whose fame is ever bright!
Glory to him, Prachet's holy son!
Whose pure lips quaff with ever-new delight
The nectar-sea of deeds by Ráma done.

Hail, arch-ascetic, pious, good, and kind!
Hail, Saint Válmíki, lord of every lore!
Hail, holy Hermit, calm and pure of mind!
Hail, First of Bards, Válmíki, hail once more!

CHAPTER 1

THE CITY OF AYODHYA

AN ELDERLY SADHU DRESSED in cotton loincloth and leaning on a wooden staff, stood on the bank of the wide, meandering Sarayu River, gazing across at the golden turrets of Ayodhya as they gleamed and shimmered in the sunlight.

The city of Ayodhya, the fortress capitol of the Kingdom of Kosala, ninety-six miles long and twenty-four miles wide, sat surrounded by a moat system, protected on all sides by walls fifty feet thick and eighty feet high, with watchtowers and canons placed at intervals, giving it an air of impregnability, while huge gates, fitted with massive bolts, guarded against attack.

Ayodhya's lofty, multi-storied Vedic style palaces were adorned with gems and precious stones, and surrounding the beautiful marble buildings were citadels, gardens, lakes, and fountains, while peacocks strutted in shady groves. The crops were plentiful, and the city's inhabitants, rich and noble. The streets, strewn with flowers, and sprinkled with scented water, were peaceful, and prosperity reigned within the pleasant boundaries of the Kingdom. Ayodhya was regarded the place perfect for meditation and serious study of the ancient Vedic texts and craft.

The center point of Ayodhya was the enormous marble Royal Palace, within which was situated a sumptuously decorated throne room under a Vedic domed roof supported up by gargantuan columns with an eternal flame burning in one corner.

Beyond the River Sarayu, across the horizon as far as the eye could see, stretched the Dandaka Forest, the largest collection of trees on earth.

The ruler of Kosala was King Dasarath, a wise, God-fearing king, coming from a long line of monarchs descended from the Solar Dynasty.

On this particular day, Dasarath, a tall, benevolent, good-natured leader with long silver hair and ocean blue eyes, sat on his elaborately decorated throne consulting with his eight ministers. Dasarath; a picture of righteousness personified; was very much loved by all the people of Ayodhya.

To assist running the country, Dasarath also relied on great priests, such as Vasishtha and Visvamitra, from whom he took advice on matters pertaining to the religious rituals and rites of that great city, and ministerial advisors who saw to it that the city's granaries and treasuries were always full.

Even so, on this day, Minister Ashoka was clearly disturbed.

"Majesty, I don't think we should send such a small force," he said, frowning.

"Do not worry Ashoka," Dasarath replied, "they are my elite troops, and have proven their worth against these demons before."

A commander entered the throne room, and approached the King, bowing low.

"Your Majesty, the army has been blessed and is ready to march."

"Very good. Take your men and proceed with the utmost haste to our border with the Dandaka Forest. You know what to do."

The commander spun on his heels and left, as Ministers Sumantra and Vijaya entered the throne room.

"Your majesty, I see the army is about to leave," said Sumantra. "Let us hope this time we are not too late. Those flesh-eaters attack, then vanish into thin air before we know it."

"Yes, Sumantra," the king replied gravely, *Rakshas* activity is on the increase. Sometimes I wonder why we have to put up with all of this, but our villages must be protected at all costs."

"When will it ever end, your majesty?" said Vijaya nervously.

"When the times change, Vijaya," Dasarath replied, walking to a nearby window, "when the times change."

He looked out and saw a battalion of sleek troops in their battledress, with the distinctive Solar Dynasty insignia emblazoned across their tunics and pennants, standing in the courtyard. Dasarath saw the commander give instructions to a Captain, who turned smartly, and ordered the troops to advance through the city gates and onto the dusty road towards the Dandaka forest.

***

Two hours later, the army waited in total silence in a clearing, enveloped in a mist so thick that, in the fading light, little could be seen.

"Keep tight," the commander ordered. "We must finish them before the light goes. You know their power increases at night."

Seeing a vague shape moving through the mist, one of the infantrymen cried, "Over there! Over there in the…"

A flash of light, followed by a scream, and the infantryman fell dead just as two figures materialized out of the gloom, Ravan, King of the Rakshas, a huge, bull of a man, with a thick black beard and dark, mean staring eyes, and his son Indrajit, a tall, lean, warrior, with a personality that matched his hawk-like face.

"Father," he said, "shall we attack?"

"Yes, Indrajit," Ravan replied, "send in the half-breeds."

Shapeless forms stepped out of the mist, appearing in their true ghastly rakshas forms, half-human and half wild beast.

Taking the army by surprise, the half-breeds attacked with sabers. The army fired back, but the rakshas moved forward, unrelenting, wading into the ranks of horrified soldiers, firing, slicing, stabbing, and killing.

"Fall back! Fall back!" shouted the commander, as a rocket exploded nearby, severing his leg below the knee.

Screaming in agony, he crumpled to the ground, as the army was forced back into thick undergrowth.

"Form up and defend!" he ordered. "Quickly!"

But as they desperately tried to regain their line, the rakshas rushed them. Two soldiers pulled the commander to safety just as the line broke, after which it was every man for himself. As the troops scattered, the rakshas came through, firing calmly and deliberately. Soldiers screamed and fell, their faces gruesome masks. A minute later a *vimana* aircraft arrived and fired on the rakshas, burning them to ashes.

The mist slowly cleared, revealing scores of dead soldiers and piles of smoking demon corpses. As for the rakshas, they had disappeared.

"Retrieve the dead. Come on, lads, quickly now!" the captain ordered.

From the shadows, Ravan watched them leave, carrying their dead and wounded, a look of complete contempt on his face. "One day, I'll wipe their entire empire off the face of the earth!" he told his son. "This I swear!"

CHAPTER 2

DASARATH'S DESIRE

DEEP IN THOUGHT, DASARATH slowly paced Ayodhya's expansive throne room, his footsteps echoing on the marble floor. As he passed the eternal flame for the third time, three ladies entered, dressed in colorful saris. Queen Kausalya, the eldest, with her warm motherly glow and full figure, walked beside Queen Sumitra, slim and dark, followed by the youngest, Kaikeyi.

The Queens approached Dasarath, and bowed respectfully.

"Ah, Queen Kausalya… Sumitra… Kaikeyi," said Dasarath.

"Greetings, my husband," said Sumitra.

Kausalya moved close to Dasarath, and took his arm as she joined him in his pacing.

"My husband," she said, "You look tired. I hope you're getting enough rest."

"I try, Kausalya," he replied, "but with state affairs and governmental matters to take care of, not to mention our patrols in the Dandaka Forest to worry about, rest is difficult."

"You shouldn't overwork yourself, my husband," Kausalya said. "What would we do if you took ill? Besides, I know you well and I am certain something else is bothering you."

Dasarath paused, "No, no," he protested. "There is nothing."

"My husband, how long have we been married?"

Dasarath looked out the window and took a deep breath.

"I am ruler of Ayodhya, the richest land in the realm," he said in a low voice. "I have three wonderful wives, six good ministers, unlimited wealth, and happy citizens. Yet, I do not have sons."

"Have faith, my husband," Sumitra said, "The Dynasty is in good hands."

"But will my Queens give me sons! I need sons to protect Kosala! In the Dandaka, Ravan's influence is getting stronger. If I do not have sons..."

"Do not fret, dear," Kausalya told him. "I'm sure something will happen soon. The good Lord will look after us."

"The good Lord has been neglecting us lately," Kaikeyi said, interrupting them.

"Kaikeyi, show some respect," Sumitra chided her.

"That's right, pick on me, just because I'm the youngest," the girl said, turning her back on them.

"Now, now, Kaikeyi," Sumitra said, slipping an arm around her shoulders, "don't start the day with a sulk."

"Don't mind Kaikeyi," Kausalya told the king, "she's just a little sensitive that's all."

The following day, after completing his morning puja, Dasarath entered the throne room and found it in chaos. Councilors and advisors shouted and argued with each other, and came to plead with him directly only to be ushered away by ministers trying to restore calm. Taking his seat on the throne, Dasarath watched impassively over the proceedings until, when disorder broke out again, he raised one hand. "Gentlemen! Gentlemen! Please!" he continued as the uproar subsided. "Citizens of Ayodhya, I know how you all feel, but it is imperative we perform this ritual in order to continue the dynasty."

As the protests started again, Ministers Siddhartha and Jayanta approached the throne.

"Your majesty," pleaded Siddhartha, "this *yajna* has not been performed for over 3,000 solar years."

"We are not sure if it'll bring good luck or bad, sire," Jayanta added.

"I need sons, Jayanta, not protests," Dasarath insisted. "If I do not get sons, the Dynasty will fail."

The debating increased, and this time, as all Dasarath's eight ministers tried to restore calm once again, Dasarath held up his hand for silence. "Citizens of Ayodhya, do you want the Solar Dynasty to continue?" he boomed, "or would you rather let it rot and die? Don't you agree that everything should be done to maintain it? Every action we perform in this material world has risk attached. But for the Dynasty, we should risk everything. Therefore I sanction a yajna. And I will not be denied."

Dasarath summoned a figure from the back. The crowd parted, revealing the Royal astrologer, a young looking man with a long white beard, wearing a purple gown covered in stars, and a flat lopsided hat decorated with peacock feathers. In one hand he held a leather bound tome.

Minister Ashok leaned towards the king.

"Your Majesty, surely you don't intend to place the future of the Dynasty in the hands of a mere astrologer?" he whispered.

"This is no ordinary astrologer, Ashok," replied Dasarath. "As you will recall, he correctly predicted our greatest battle against the Rakshas, thereby preventing a terrible disaster."

"Let him come," Ashok shouted as Dasarath waved.

"Your Majesty," the astrologer said, humbly approaching the throne, "I need to appease everyone concerning the forthcoming sacrifice, and must emphasize that on occasions like these, a proper astrological reading should be undertaken if the outcome is to be successful."

"Tell us then, what is the opinion of the stars?" asked Dasarath.

"Your Majesty, according to the Vedic astrological chart, this is a superb time to perform a yajna. The planets are auspiciously placed, predicting great good fortune. For maximum beneficial results, however, according to the *Artharva Veda*, the *Ashvamedha* yajna must be performed promptly at noon, tomorrow."

"Then make immediate arrangements for the yajna!" Dasarath announced, then, turning to a minister. "Sumantra, inform Rishyasringa to begin preparations for the ceremony at dawn."

Minister Mantrapala looked at Ministers Dhriti and Arthasadaka.

"I hope our gracious Majesty gets the sons he desires," Minister Mantrapala muttered. "Otherwise it will be the end of us, and Ravan will take over the whole world."

CHAPTER 3

THE YAJNA

THE THRONE ROOM, THICK with incense, and decorated with flags and bunting, was filled to capacity with *rishis*, ministers, counselors, visiting kings, and dignitaries, together with all the people of Ayodhya.

In the center, a hundred golden pots were placed around a large sacrificial fire, which was surrounded by a rectangle of six octagonal pillars, forty–two feet high, spaced four feet apart, plated with polished gold and decorated with silken cloths and garlands of flowers. Dasarath's throne was fashioned in the shape of a huge Garuda, the swan carrier of Lord *Vishnu*.

Around the fire sat sage Rishyasringa, assisted by half a dozen Brahmins who glowed with absolute purity, along with three senior councilors, Suyagnya, Jabali and Kashyapa.

Ringing a little bell, Rishyasringa poured clarified butter onto the fire, all the while chanting ancient Vedic *Sanskrit mantras*.

Servants, wearing the red livery of the royal house, stood with silver bowls full of gold, jewels and herbs, while female servants dressed in yellow cloth carried garlands of white flowers, pots of honey and clarified butter. To one side, a chariot, draped in expensive purple fabric, stood opposite a contingent of foot soldiers armed with swords. On the other side stood elephants marked with auspicious signs, and a bull with gilded horns.

After a few minutes of chanting, the fire started to burn brighter, flames leaping into the air, turning green and yellow, and suddenly, out of it's midst stepped an angelic being with hair like molten gold. Dressed in crimson silk, adorned with glittering ornaments, and blazing like the midday sun, he illuminated the whole room with his effulgence.

The chanting faltered, and the Brahmins leapt to their feet, spilling holy water. Dishes of rice upturned, scattering grains everywhere. In the background, someone screamed.

Dasarath half rose off the throne, as, one by one, the townsfolk fell to the floor, offering their obeisances.

Producing a golden bowl with a silver lid, the angel smiled, and approached Dasarath, who, while shielding his eyes from the brightness, got stiffly to his feet.

"King Dasarath," the angel said, "I come on behalf of Lord Vishnu, the Supreme Personality of Godhead. Being well pleased with your worship, He sends this vessel containing payasa, the nectar of the gods. Let the queens drink, and they shall bear fruit."

Dasarath slowly took the bowl, and held it up, turning to the congregation. When he turned back, the angel had gone. Dasarath looked around in confusion.

"Clear the court," an official shouted, as Dasarath stepped down from the throne.

"Sumantra," whispered Dasarath, beckoning his minister, "inform me when the queens are in my private quarters."

Dasarath entered his sumptuously furnished room, lined with bookcases on three sides, filled with gold embossed volumes.

Along with his three queens, sitting before a fire on plump pillows, was Manthara, Kaikeyi's old maidservant, her grotesque hunchback protruding under her black clothes.

Sumitra and Kaikeyi watched as Dasarath approached Kausalya with the bowl.

"Kausalya," he said, "we have been blessed. Drink this nectar and by the grace of the gods, you will conceive."

Kausalya looked at Dasarath in surprise. This was new to her, but Dasarath had spoken.

"Pray and show your gratitude," he added as Kausalya handed him back the bowl.

Then Kausalya bowed her head while Sumitra and Kaikeyi looked expectantly at him.

"And now, Sumitra, you must drink." said Dasarath, pushing the bowl at her.

Sumitra took it in both hands and drank.

"Pray and show gratitude."

As Dasarath approached Kaikeyi, Manthara straightened up, her eyes burning.

"We are blessed this day. Please drink," said Dasarath, offering Kaikeyi the bowl. After she sipped the nectar, Manthara leaned across and whispered in her ear.

"Remember this day, my Queen."

And when she too, had prayed, he turned to Sumitra and told her to take what was left, before retiring to his private chamber.

***

Four Princes were born to the wives of Dasarath, and tradition dictated that the king distribute gifts to the musicians and performers in the street, and gold and cows to the holy men. The city became a noisy hub of activity, the streets crowded with artists, actors, singers and monks chanting mystic mantras, praising the Lord's holy name.

On the eleventh night after the birth of the royal sons, the lights in the palace nursery blazed into the darkness. Through the narrow windows leading councilors could be seen gathered with the Royal family for the Prince's name giving ceremony. Dasarath, overcome with joy, fussed continually over his sons, walking back and forth between their cribs, looking into their perfect little faces and playing with their tiny fingers.

When the family priests entered – Vasishtha, holding a large book, and Vamadeva, with a jar of nectar – Sumitra and Kaikeyi hugged their babies while Dasarath smiled and laughed, the proud father at last, of four healthy sons.

Visvamitra, teacher and guru of Ayodhya, sporting a perfectly manicured silver beard, his gently smiling face reflecting a life of deep learning and austerity, stood next to Dasarath, and asked Vamadeva to administer the nectar to the infants. While Vasishtha recited Sanskrit verses from the book, Visvamitra placed a hand on the head of each of Sumitra's babies, as Vamadeva dipped a silver spoon into the jar.

"Sumitra, I name your sons Lakshman and Shatrughna," he exclaimed, "May they both grow strong and healthy."

Everyone cheered as the names were announced and Vamadeva fed each child a spoonful of the liquid. Sumitra cuddled her boys as Visvamitra moved on to a delighted Kaikeyi, who cradled her dark-complexioned child in her arms, rocking him gently. Beside her, as always, stood her faithful servant, Manthara.

"Kaikeyi, I name your son, Bharat. May he grow strong and healthy."

"Oh, Manthara, isn't Bharat a wonderful name?" she said proudly as the cheers rang out again.

"Yes, my lady," said Manthara, patting Bharat on the head. "And one day, our little Prince can also be a king," she added in a whisper.

Visvamitra crossed to Kausalya, who picked up her dark complexion child from his crib. He was a little different, special.

"Kausalya," said Visvamitra, "your son's name will be Ram. May he grow strong and healthy."

"Ram!" said an onlooker.

"A great name!" exclaimed another.

This time Vasishtha administered the nectar himself, as Kausalya gazed lovingly at her black-haired son's beautiful face.

"Oh, Ram," she said softly, "I am the happiest mother in the kingdom."

Later that night, on a windswept parapet high above the palace, stood Manthara, arms outstretched towards the Pole Star.

"Bharat will be king!" she screeched ominously into the howling wind. "I will make sure of that!"

CHAPTER 4

THE SONS OF DASARATH

KING DASARATH FELT MUCH better. Now that he had his much-desired sons, gone was the melancholy that had dogged him for so long, replaced as it was by the bliss of fatherhood. The kingdom now stood a chance in the continuing war against Ravan.

The heavenly potion drunk by the Queens had contributed to the fact that all the royal sons were born beautiful, strong, and well behaved. As they got older, they grew tall, handsome and virtuous, all of them studious and wise, and became very much attached to one another.

Though Ram and Lakshman were born of different mothers, they were totally inseparable. As a baby, Ram would not sleep till Lakshman was brought to lie beside him. They played, worked, and studied together, spending every waking moment in each other's company. Over time, Lakshman accepted his role as protector of the half-brother who he recognized as his master. Shatrughna and Bharat also bonded, and would often pit themselves against Ram and Lakshman in sport.

The Princes also exhibited great aptitude in learning the art of warfare, yet remained humble, righteous, and respectful to their elders. They were gentle and honest, and very dear to everyone. As they grew from boyhood, to youth, to young men, their prowess, bravery, and expert bowmanship became known throughout the Kingdom of Kosala.

***

One day, Bharat and Shatrughna, having reached fifteen years, were sparring with wooden swords in the palace garden, under the watchful eye of their teacher, Vasishtha.

"Come on Bharat!" Lakshman shouted from the sidelines, "you can do better than that. In the guts Shatrughna! In the guts!"

"Whose side are you on, Lakshman?" protested Bharat.

When Dasarath arrived to observe his sons, Vasishtha, amused by the mistakes that they still made, joined him. Dasarath eyed his sons critically.

"Vasishtha, how are the Princes coming along?" Dasarath asked.

"Their speed with which they learn is phenomenal, Majesty." whispered Vasishtha. "Your sons already have the characters of saints. They can control the six passions of lust, anger, greed, infatuation, pride and jealousy. They can drive a chariot, fight, and shoot their arrows like veterans. They really don't need teaching now since they seem to know everything already, especially Ram. It's as if he…"

"Look, here is Ram now," hissed Dasarath, noting how he was changing into a husky young man. "Ram, how are you today, my son?"

"Very well, father," Ram told him as he walked up, hugging his father affectionately.

Dasarath looked into Ram's eyes with deep love and affection, "You'll make me proud when you become a warrior Prince," he said.

"I will dedicate each and every day of my life to please you, father."

"Your broad shoulders have yet to feel the weight of the world," Vasishtha told the youth. "I have a feeling, when that time comes, you will be ready."

Thanking him, Ram strolled over to a nearby fountain.

"Watching them makes my heart leap with joy," Dasarath whispered, as Bharat grabbed Ram, and playfully tried to wrestle him to the ground.

"I count my blessings every day," sighed Dasarath. "My four wonderful sons."

"There you go again, Bharat," laughed Shatrughna, as Bharat hit the dust.

"Ram's the champ!" Lakshman shouted.

"All right," Ram said, grinning, as he disengaged himself. "That's enough for one day."

"Why don't you spend as much time with us as you did before?" Shatrughna asked him.

"Brother, don't you realize our kingdom is under constant threat? We must be vigilant," Ram told him earnestly. "An attack could come at any time. Please try to take your training seriously."

"No one in their right mind would attack us while you're around," said Shatrughna.

"And what if I left Ayodhya?"

Bharat, Lakshman and Shatrughna looked at each other in surprise, while Vasishtha and Dasarath studied Ram closely.

"Ram is such a serious boy nowadays," said Dasarath, "I put it down to growing up."

"Ram will live an important life, Your Majesty," said Vasishtha, "one of great significance. His name will be remembered for millennia to come."

Bharat and Shatrughna were inseparable, and just like Ram and Lakshman; fine princes. But, Ram was their role model, moral and even minded, compassionate, courageous, and true to his word. Ram was the controller of his senses, a sage of high learning, an upholder of *dharma*, and a great warrior skilled in the art of archery and combat, dearer to his father than the others, and one day, destined to become the perfect ruler of a perfect land.

Vasishtha walked across to Ram and instructed him to begin practice. As Dasarath watched, Ram picked up his bow, and nodded to an assistant, who spun a circular target dotted with holes. He slipped an arrow onto the bow, took aim and fired. The arrow missed the target but Vasishtha urged him to try again.

This time, the arrow zipped through a hole in the target, and then lost itself in the bushes.

"And one day Ram is going to protect us all!" Lakshman taunted him, hands on hips.

The brothers all laughed heartily, including Vasishtha.

Ram, unperturbed, fired again, and this time, his arrow found the center.

"That's it!" shouted Vasishtha, as the brothers cheered Ram's effort.

Meanwhile, someone else was showing a great interest in the princes. Hidden in the bushes, Manthara, who had croaked with delight as Ram's arrow missed the target, spat in disgust when it hit the bulls-eye.

"One day his luck will run out!" she hissed.

CHAPTER 5

SAGE VISVAMITRA

DAPPLED SUNLIGHT STREAMED DOWN through the trees onto a narrow trail, on a still, warm day, deep in the Dandaka forest. A squirrel stood on hind legs to listen, and then scampered up a tree, as, in the distance, something could be heard crashing through the bushes, followed by a yell.

A haggard Visvamitra appeared, struggling through the undergrowth, stopping to catch his breath on reaching the trail. As he staggered on, a number of large, black, wasp-like creatures darted at him, making him duck and weave.

When one swooped down with such force that he was knocked to the ground, he crashed into the bushes and lay still.

"Those demons," he groaned, "will they ever give up?"

After a few minutes of quiet, Visvamitra picked himself up and ran as fast as he could down a path lined with trees and bushes that took on a new life as he passed, viciously snapping and flicking their branches at him. One large branch knocked him to the ground where he lay sprawled, breathing hard; until, once again, all was quiet.

Pushing on, he reached a clearing and saw the welcome sight of Ayodhya in the distance.

Quickly, he reached the familiar drawbridge spanning the green water, and scurried along to the main gate where he was admitted by a startled guard. Crossing the courtyard, he passed battalions of elite troopers, and was spotted by a herald, who ran to tell the king.

Dasarath lit up when he heard, "Visvamitra is here?" he cried, "that is indeed good news."

As the sage entered, the king descended the throne with his wives, and greeted him warmly.

"Visvamitra, you're back," he said. "Your visit, as usual, is a blessing on this house, and, as you know, I will continue to support you in all your endeavors. But you are clearly in a state, revered sage. Tell me, what is the matter?"

"Your Majesty," Visvamitra said, "I need your help. The forest is not a safe place anymore. At our ashram in the Dandaka, our ceremonies and sacred rites are constantly attacked by rakshas! It is beyond my power to stop this desecration!"

"Ravan again!" Dasarath said grimly.

Off to one side, standing in a doorway, a tall and broad-shouldered youth, dressed in yellow cloth, and carrying a bow, watched the proceedings with interest. His high cheekbones and beautiful gait gave him the countenance of an emperor. A yellow band was wrapped around his waist, golden pennants hung from his ears, while a string of pearls, together with a tiger claw, and a necklace of gems including a large diamond, dangled from his neck. On a finger sat an exquisite signet ring. Vaisnava tilak adorned his brow, and a loop of yellow Brahmin thread was slung across his left shoulder and under his right arm.

"Yes, Majesty," said Visvamitra, "Ravan is again ordering his henchmen to disturb our holy men in the forest. There is only one option left. You must send Ram to deal with them."

Dasarath paled, while Kausalya fell against Sumitra in a swoon. In the doorway, Ram smiled.

"Never!" Dasarath declared, "Ram is no more than a boy, no match for the ogres who fight without rules, whose strength increases by night. I will send my army instead, but do not ask for Ram. I could not bear to be parted from him, not even for a moment."

"By the gods!" Visvamitra cried, "you agreed to assist me, now you break your word! A king's word is his bond, and yet you break yours in an instant! I shall go."

"Father," Ram said, as he joined him, "Visvamitra is right. It is my duty to fight these demons. Besides," he added with a smirk, "I could do with a little practice."

"No, Ram!" his father cried, "No!"

"Spiritual *dharma* is the most important aspect of our culture, Your Majesty," Vasishtha said, entering the room, "and must be upheld. Ayodhya is the center of dharma, and you, our king, its father. Ram has yet to prove himself. How can this happen if he remains at home. He has the touch of divinity and will be well protected. Let him go. It is his destiny."

"Very well," Dasarath conceded after a long silence, "but only on one condition. His brother, Lakshman, must accompany him."

"As you wish."

"Visvamitra," a distraught Kausalya begged, "please bring my son back in one piece!"

"It is the will of the gods," Visvamitra replied, "and therefore out of my hands," at which both Kausalya and Sumitra collapsed in tears.

CHAPTER 6

TRIAL IN THE FOREST

THE NEXT MORNING, RAM and Lakshman followed Visvamitra along a dim trail through the Dandaka forest, each carrying a large bow.

"Let us rest here for a while," Visvamitra told them, taking a roll of parchment from his robe and handing it to Ram. "These are ancient mantras needed to invoke, dispatch and withdraw certain *Astra* weapons. After you memorize them, show them to Lakshman." And sinking to the ground, he closed his eyes while the two youths studied the parchment he had handed them. Neither said a word as they exchanged glances.

"What do these rakshas demons look like?" Lakshman asked Ram, when they were back on the trail heading deeper into the forest.

"From what I've heard, they're not a pretty sight." Ram replied, looking around. "This is a strange forest."

"I'm beginning to notice," said Lakshman nervously. "How long before we see them?"

"We're near the ashram," whispered Visvamitra, "we should be quiet."

As they approached the sage's encampment, a high-pitched scream ripped through the air.

"What was that?" Lakshman gasped, twisting around.

"They're here!" Visvamitra hissed. "Quick! Follow me!"

A moment later, they entered a wide clearing, and saw monks shaking their fists at two fierce looking creatures with gnarled, black faces and sharp claws, hovering above the encampment, dropping blood and bones onto a large fire.

"Get away! Get away with you!" shouted a monk.

"Be gone!" cried another.

The demons, laughing hideously, dropped more bones onto the fire.

Ram turned to Visvamitra. "Master," he said, "what shall we do?"

"You must use your bow to dispatch them, Ram," the sage replied, as he started to chant mantras for their protection.

Ram brought his bow to the ready, loaded an arrow, and pulled back the bowstring. Taking aim at the nearest demon, he released the arrow, which exploded against a nearby tree. The demons spotted them.

"What have you done?" Lakshman cried.

"Quick, Ram," Visvamitra urged, "another arrow!"

But as Ram tried to reload, one of the demons closed fast, knocking him to the ground, while a second screamed in, bowling over Lakshman. A moment later, the brothers were forced deeper into the soft earth as the demons returned, roaring overhead. The first one circled again, and started straight at Ram, who quickly picked himself up and fired an arrow, blasting the demon across the sky. Its dying wail rang out across the clearing.

"Look, Ram! There's more!" shouted Visvamitra, as a horde of them appeared.

Ram fired again and again, blasting the rakshas back and upwards until the remaining demons fled.

"Ram, you're unbeatable!" Lakshman cried triumphantly.

"I hope they don't come back," said Ram, looking up at the sky.

"You have great potential, Ram," said Visvamitra. "We should be safe now."

Bidding the monks farewell, the brothers followed Visvamitra to his hut, where they sat on the floor listening to him chanting. After a few minutes, Visvamitra spoke.

"After your experience with the dark forces, I'm sure you will find this next trial of interest," he said, looking at Ram. "King Janak of Videha is organizing a bow-lifting competition in Mithila. He has invited many young princes from kingdoms far and wide to test their strength. Many men and demons have tried to raise this gigantic bow, which has never been lifted nor strung. Would you like to go?"

"If it would please you, *gurudeva*," said Ram humbly, while Lakshman nodded in approval.

"Rest then," Visvamitra told them, "We leave at first light."

"What would happen if you lifted that bow," Lakshman asked later, as he lay beside Ram. He saw the answer in his brother's shining eyes.

CHAPTER 7

CONTEST IN MITHILA

AFTER A FEW DAYS travel, Visvamitra and the princes reached Mithila, and made their way to the palace, where they met King Janak, an aging monarch with flowing white beard and a soft, kind face, accompanied by the family priest, Satananda, and chief counselor, Sudaman.

"My dear Visvamitra, how good it is to see you again! Welcome!" cried the King.

"Your Majesty, this is Ram and Lakshman, sons of King Dasarath of Ayodhya."

"Ah! Dasarath's sons. How you have grown. Welcome to Mithila, you are just in time. I have arranged a competition to see who can lift and string *Haradhanu,* the mighty bow of Lord Siva, which, long ago, was given to King Devarata, a monarch in our family line. Many heroes have attempted to lift and string it, yet, in all this time no one has been able to raise it one inch. Many princes have come from far and wide today, so we will have a great show. You both may try if you wish," he added, looking at the princes.

"Thank you, your majesty," Lakshman said, "but Ram must go first, Sire."

"Good luck then, Ram," said Janak, as he left them and strolled towards the royal box.

A plucky boy who followed them into the courtyard, tugged at Ram's tunic.

"Are you going to lift the great bow of Siva?" he asked. "They say that whoever succeeds will be given the king's daughter in marriage. See! There she is on the balcony, watching. Her name is Sita."

Raising his eyes, Ram saw a young girl leaning against a pillar. And indeed, she was beautiful with her peach smooth skin, dark sparkling eyes, and jet-black hair hanging down to her waist.

Ram found it difficult removing his gaze from her.

"And there is her sister, Urmila," the boy said eagerly. "And behind her stand Mandavi and Srutakirti, daughters of King Janak's brother."

Ram noticed Sita looking down towards them, and then staring intently at him.

The sound of strident trumpets and the thunder of kettledrums announced the start of the contest, and Lakshman made his way to the seating area, followed by Ram, who was still looking at the loveliest girl he had ever seen.

King Janak and Queen Sunayana, a dark beauty, sat in the royal box, surrounded by ministers, officials, courtiers, servants and ladies-in-waiting. The public galleries were crammed with townsfolk; and those without seats filled all available space on roofs and walls around the courtyard.

A fanfare sounded, and a heavy velvet curtain was dragged back, to expose an enormous bow set on an eight-wheeled cart, and indeed it was a formidable sight, four feet in diameter, covered in an intricate design and draped with garlands of flowers. The crowd gasped. The bow was the size of a large tree trunk!

Sita was leaning over the balcony now, watching Ram intently, as the other girls gathered excitedly around her. An official rose to his feet, and the crowd fell silent.

"Today, in Mithila, courtesy of King Janak, the great bow of Lord Siva is now displayed," the official announced. "This ancient bow has never been strung. Those who desire to lift the bow will have their chance today. Let the contest begin," continued the official.

A giant, lantern-jawed prince with barrel chest and bulging biceps stepped up, powerful muscles rippling as he took his stance. The Prince flexed his body, and slipped his huge arms under the bow. He grimaced and attempted to lift it, but no matter how hard he heaved and pushed, it would not budge. He puffed and blew, struggled and strained, turning a dozen shades of purple, but the bow remained tightly in place. He tried one final time, but without success. Giving up in disgust, he swaggered off; head held high, sweat pouring down his powerful body. Thereafter, prince after prince tried, but failed to lift the bow, and after the last prince left the podium, the official looked down his list again.

"The Prince Ram of Ayodhya," he announced.

High on the balcony, Sita breathed Ram's name when he stood up.

Ram stepped up, offered his respects to the bow, and positioned himself for the lift. Running his hand lightly along the surface, feeling its contours, he closed his eyes and bowed, and, as the courtyard fell silent, clasped his hands together in prayer.

"That Prince Ram is a handsome one," Queen Sunayana whispered to the king. "If he lifts the bow, our daughter will get a fine husband."

Everyone watched in silence as Ram slowly slid his left hand under the bow, feeling its smooth polished surface. He took a deep breath, braced himself, and pushed up.

Nothing.

Ram took another deep breath and pushed up with all his strength. Still nothing. He looked uncertain, and glanced at Lakshman, who was watching him anxiously. A ripple of excitement ran through the crowd. Some stood to get a better view, one or two shouted encouragement.

"You have one more try left," said the official.

Ram was perplexed. Then a look of realization crossed his face. He relaxed, and prepared to try again with renewed determination. He pushed again, and very s-l-o-w-l-y, the bow began to move. The whole arena held its breath.

Ram exerted more pressure, and then pushed up again. This time, the bow rose gracefully out of the cradle.

A great sigh emanated from the crowd. Suddenly, everyone was on their feet, roaring their approval.

Above the crowd, Sita clutched the railing of the balcony, looking on in amazement.

And now Ram was pushing the bow skywards, locking his arms, and everyone was shouting and cheering, yelling and screaming. When Ram half-turned, holding the bow high above his head, the crowds went wild and Sita clapped her hands.

Then Ram slowly placed the bow on its end, and picked up the bowstring lying on the ground.

"He's going to string it!" shouted a citizen. "He's going to string the bow!"

Holding the bow in his left hand, Ram attached the string, and started to bend it with his right hand. People gasped in disbelief as the bow creaked, the ground shook, and fixtures rattled and fell off the walls. Then, Ram bent the bow further, as he attempted to loop the string over the end. Suddenly, the bow snapped clean in half, and a thunderous roar reverberated round the courtyard. Visvamitra and Janak steadied themselves, Sita was thrown back on a bench and Lakshman nearly fell. Everyone else was knocked to the ground by the shockwave.

Janak hugged his wife, crying like a child. Visvamitra prayed to the heavens, and Urmila gave Sita a big hug.

Picking up one half of the bow, Ram held it jubilantly above his head.

"Citizens of Mithila," King Janak cried, getting to his feet, "nothing like this has ever happened before. An age-old tradition has been broken! A royal prince has lifted the great bow of Siva. As a consequence, it is with great pleasure, I announce, Prince Ram of

Ayodhya will take the hand of my daughter, Sita, in marriage."

The crowd broke into cheers again as, holding up a large piece of the bow, Ram looked up at Sita, who clasped both hands over her mouth. And in that moment, their fates became entwined as one.

CHAPTER 8

A ROYAL WEDDING

A FEW DAYS LATER, members of the Ayodhya Royal family, and their ministers, arrived in Mithila. Alighting from his carriage, King Dasarath, together with Bharat and Shatrughna, went straight to the palace in search of his sons, and found them in a courtyard together with Sita and her sisters.

"My dear Ram, may you be blessed," an elated Dasarath cried, "and Sita, my dear, welcome to the Royal House of the *Ishvakus*. I pray you have a happy life together. Long may you live."

"Thank you, father," said Ram.

"Ram, I always thought you were a winner," shouted Bharat.

Shatrughna grabbed Ram by the shoulder, while Bharat embraced Lakshman. Only then did he notice Mandavi and Srutakirti standing nearby. "Bharat," he hissed, "do my eyes deceive me?"

"No brother, your eyes are perfect," replied Bharat, looking at the sisters.

"My dear Dasarath," King Janaka announced, sweeping into the courtyard, his robes billowing behind him. "It is an honor and a privilege to be linked with the house of the Solar Dynasty."

"Likewise, Janak," Dasarath replied.

"This is the beginning of good times," Janak said, smiling warmly.

The very next day, the marriage of Ram and Sita, and also of those of Lakshman to Urmila, Bharat to Mandevi and Shatrughna to Srutakirti, took place in the colorfully decorated throne room in King Janak's Palace.

After the ceremony, Ram and Sita walked slowly towards the main door, followed by the brothers and their respective brides. The lovely Sita looked like a goddess from the heavenly planets, her dark hair done up in braids and decorated with white flowers. Jewels adorned her body, and she wore a gorgeous red sari. Ram, the prince among princes, attired in a nuptial gown, muscular body anointed with aromatic oils and spices, gleamed in the morning light.

They posed in the enormous palace doorway, and drew a tumultuous roar from onlookers, who showered them with flowers.

After the ceremony, lavishly decorated chariots drawn by white horses conveyed the princes and their wives back to Ayodhya.

For the people of Mithila and Ayodhya, that day would be remembered for a long time to come.

As deep as the ocean, as lasting as the mountains, the love between Ram and Sita, a real, transcendental, eternal love, eclipsed all mundane relationships between men and women.

Ram and Sita spent many days in each other's company, walking together through the shady groves in the palace gardens, listening to the colorful peacocks singing their songs from the branches of the flowering cherry trees, or quietly sitting beside the crystal clear lakes and tanks, watching the flocks of geese and families of beautiful swans. For the couple, life was as sweet as nectar, and as time passed, they became more and more attracted to each other, their love expanding with a radiant purity, binding them together for all time.

Ram, befitting the warrior he was, spent part of his days practicing archery and studying the art of warfare, learning the ways of the world from his teachers and elders, gradually he became more and more like his father, kindhearted to everyone he met, patient and humble. Not only that, but he had great respect for the opinions of others, and gave sound and practical advice to those whose paths he crossed. Sita was also busy, her many royal duties within the palace, helping with the children, welcoming visiting royalty, and assisting at official receptions, taking up a lot of her time.

Some would say Ram, being instructed in the ways of government and royal etiquette, was being groomed to take over as king when his father gave up the throne, but that seemed a long way off.

As the years rolled by, and Dasarath's days increased in number, the aging monarch eventually realized that a decision regarding retirement from active rule would have to be made. How much longer he would go on living, he did not know, but one thing was for certain, he must decide on a successor.

***

One day, King Ashvapati of Kaikeya, father of Queen Kaikeyi, sent for Prince Bharat. Dasarath immediately consented, and at Bharat's request, allowed Shatrughna to accompany his brother.

In the palace courtyard, Bharat and Shatrughna mounted two saddled horses, as Mandavi and Srutakirti ran to join them, followed at a leisurely pace, by Sita, Ram, Lakshman, and the Queens.

"Safe journey," Ram shouted, as they backed their horses. "Give our love to Yudhajit and grandfather."

"See you all soon," shouted Bharat.

"Good luck," said Lakshman, and everyone waved as Bharat and Shatrughna rode off.

As they walked away together, Sita turned to Ram.

"Ram, do Bharat and Shatrughna have to go to grandfather's?" she asked.

"Yes," Ram replied. "King Ashvapati has requested their presence. Don't worry, Sita. They'll be back before you know it."

As they re-entered the palace Ram looked up and saw Dasarath watching from a balcony, fingering the gray hairs on his temple.

CHAPTER 9

THE NEW KING

RAM AND HIS BEAUTIFUL wife, Sita, the divine couple, often sat at their favorite spot in the palace garden, beside the fountain beneath the wandering honeysuckle and clematis. This was their little hideaway, where they came to get away the bustle of palace life. They loved the tranquility of the place, and the sweet smell of lilac and jasmine.

"It's been two months now, Ram," Sita said, leaning against his shoulder. "When will Shatrughna and Bharat be coming back? Everyone misses them."

"They will be at Kekaya for a little longer, Sita," Ram told her fondly. "Grandfather needs their company. And, as you know, he is too old to travel."

"Ram," she whispered, offering him a rose to smell. "I love you even more than when we first met."

"I feel the same way about you, Sita," said Ram, looking deeply into her dark lotus eyes.

They sat there silent after that, with the bumblebees droning among the flowers, and the little fountain splashing a few feet away, until Minister Sumantra appeared and broke the spell.

"Prince Ram, I come from your father," he said in a solemn voice. "He is requesting your company in the royal chambers. It is a matter of special importance."

Dasarath looked out of his window again. When he saw the pennant on Ram's chariot, he brightened, and made his way to the door to greet Ram and Sita.

"I want to talk with you on an important matter concerning the future of the dynasty," said Dasarath soberly, as his son walked into the room. "Please sit."

Ram and Sita took their places on the spacious couch against the wall.

"As you know, Ram," his father continued, clearing his throat, "I am not getting any younger, and I therefore feel that now is the right time to discuss this particular matter. I've already consulted my ministers, and they all agree." Dasarath looked directly at his son. "Ram, I want you to take the throne."

Ram let the words sink in before replying.

"Father, it is a great responsibility. I do not know if I am ready."

"You are ready, Ram," his father assured him, "You've been trained from birth to be a Warrior Prince. You are, honest, righteous, diplomatic, and fully conversant with the six branches of Vedic auxiliary knowledge, and the ceremonial rules and regulations of the Vedas. I don't see why you would not make a great king."

"I will try my best to follow in your footsteps, father," he said, bowing deeply.

"The Coronation will take place tomorrow," Dasarath informed him. "With the constellation Pusya in ascendant, and, the moon in conjunction, it will be most auspicious."

"Father, I am honored," Ram said earnestly, "Ayodhya is my home and I will put the people first. I will not fail you."

"I know you will make me proud," his father said, "I'll be happy to leave this mortal world knowing the kingdom is in your capable hands, and the interests of the people topmost in your mind. Now tell your mother and receive her blessings."

Ram and Sita made their way to Kausalya's apartments, and found her in the small temple room, dressed in white silks, quietly reciting Vedic mantras. Lakshman and Sumitra stood by her side.

"Mother, I have just been appointed Prince Regent," Ram declared, prostrating himself before her.

"Oh, Ram, that's wonderful news," said Kausalya, rising slowly, her eyes growing moist. "I have already been informed by one of your good friends."

"Please give me your blessings, mother," he said, rising to meet her embrace.

"Long may you live, my son," she told him. "May all your enemies be vanquished, and may all your subjects be protected and happy. When is the Coronation?"

"Tomorrow, mother."

Sumitra and Lakshman gathered round Ram and congratulated him.

"Ayodhya, indeed the whole of Kosala, will be safe in your hands, Ram," Lakshman said.

"And you, dear Sita," said Sumitra, embracing her, "will make the perfect queen."

***

Conversations roared like ocean storms through the throne room of Ayodhya as kings, ministers, priests, officers, councilors and townspeople waited to hear their king. A fanfare sounded, and Dasarath entered, his gold colored dhoti rustling against his legs, and mounted the throne, with Ram and Lakshman taking their seats on either side of him.

"Citizens of Ayodhya, I have called you here for an important announcement," Dasarath declared sternly, his firm gaze scanning the sea of faces. "I have decided to relinquish the throne."

Gasps of dismay and disbelief rippled through the assembly as townspeople exchanged shocked glances.

Looking at Ram, Dasarath continued, "But do not be disappointed, my successor has been chosen. It is my eldest son, Prince Ram!"

Instantly, the crowd jumped in the air, cheering, chanting, and roaring their approval.

"All Glories to Prince Ram!"

When Ram stood and took a little bow, the crowds erupted again, chanting his name, this time louder.

"Glories to Prince Ram!" they cried over and over again, "Glories to Prince Ram!"

CHAPTER 10

THE BOONS

SOON, NEWS OF THE Coronation spread throughout Kosala. Within hours, the city had been decorated. Flowers adorned every street, and pennants hung from every balcony along the main thoroughfares as townsfolk began to celebrate.

On the palace roof, taking in some fresh air, was Manthara. Looking at the clouds, drifting like huge cotton balls across the azure sky, she heard music. Was heaven so near? she asked herself. Was this a celestial choir? Then she realized it was coming from the street below. Looking over the parapet, she saw the decorations, and was puzzled. In great agitation, she scuttled towards the court nurse she had spotted earlier at the far end of the roof.

"What is going on?" she demanded shrilly, "Why is music playing, and why is the city decorated?"

"It's for the Coronation," the nurse replied. "Didn't you know that the king has given up the throne?"

44

"What!" gasped Manthara, turning pale.

"Tomorrow, Prince Ram will be crowned Regent."

A shocked Manthara turned, nearly tripping over her black dress, and scooted off, the shawl covering her hunchback billowing up behind her. She must tell her mistress at once.

Kaikeyi was in her quarters when the door flew open and Manthara burst in unannounced.

"Queen Kaikeyi! I have just heard…" breathing heavily, she carefully closed the door behind her. "… Some important news! The king has relinquished the throne. Ram is to be crowned Regent."

"Why, Manthara, that's wonderful!"

Kaikeyi rose from her couch, removed an expensive gold and pearl necklace from around her neck, and handed it to the old woman.

"Here, Manthara," she said, "this is for you in honor of today. Let's celebrate."

"I bring you bad news, my lady, and you give me pearls!" she screeched, snatching the necklace from Kaikeyi. Angrily screwing up her wrinkled face, she wrung her scraggily arms in the air, and dashed it to the floor, pearls and rubies scattering in all directions.

"This is the beginning of the end for us!" she cried.

"Manthara," Kaikeyi gasped, trembling to see Manthara in such a fury. "What has come over you?"

"If handled carefully," Manthara said with force, "a great opportunity will present itself."

"Is this another of your schemes?" Kaikeyi asked firmly, sitting down.

"My lady, I have known you since you were a child, I even helped in your upbringing. Do you not trust my judgment? Your son, Bharat, should be king, not Ram."

"Bharat, for king? No, it has already been decided. Ram is…"

"My queen, can't you see the evil conspiracy in the making aimed at cheating Bharat out of the crown. Do you really believe everything Dasarath says? Bharat will be banished, even put to death after Ram is crowned, and when Ram's reign is over, his sons will rule, and you will cease to exist! Soon, it will be too late! You must act at once! Force a change! If Bharat is denied the throne, Kausalya will get her greatest wish! She always wanted to usurp you and be the favorite!"

"Manthara, stop!" Kaikeyi protested. "You go too far."

"Don't you think it strange, your son absent at this crucial time?" said the old woman. "Why has he been sent away? Is he really needed at Kekaya?"

"Manthara! This is absurd! His grandfather requested that he come."

"This whole thing has been meticulously planned in favor of Ram. Bharat doesn't stand a chance."

Kaikeyi rose from her couch and stared pensively at Manthara.

"Bharat would make an excellent king, my lady," Manthara persisted. "I know you think so too."

Kaikeyi thought for a long while before replying.

"I once had a dream," Kaikeyi told her. "Bharat was sitting on the throne with a crown on his head. Everyone was throwing flower petals at him. Even Ram was bowing. It seemed so real to me."

"Dreams sometimes come true, my lady."

"I've raised Bharat from birth, Manthara. I've watched him grow into a strong and noble warrior. I…. But it has already been decided."

"No, my lady," the cunning Manthara contradicted her. "It is not too late."

"But, Manthara," Kaikeyi cried. "Even if I wanted to, how could I make sure that Bharat gets the crown? Tell me that."

Manthara rubbed her hands in glee.

"That's easy, my lady. Use the boons."

"Boons? What boons?"

"Don't you remember? Dasarath granted you two wishes. You earned them by your unselfish action on the battlefield. Had it not been for you, the King would not be alive today. It's our only chance. Insist on what is rightfully yours and install Bharat on the throne. Don't let Dasarath rob you of this chance. I will tell you what to say. Now go directly to the sulking room."

In the sulking room, Manthara removed Kaikeyi's flower tresses and jewels, and smiling sardonically, threw them on the floor, after which she unbraided Kaikeyi's beautiful hair, dressing her in black before leaving her alone with her despair. Wet with perspiration, Kaikeyi lay on the floor in great anguish.

***

Each day, Dasarath would make a point of visiting Kaikeyi. As she was the youngest, it always made him happy to see her, and he looked forward to this meeting with great anticipation.

Dasarath shuffled up to Kaikeyi's room, and tapped twice on the thick wooden door.

"Where is Queen Kaikeyi?" he asked the maid who answered it.

"She's in the sulking room, Your Majesty."

"What!"Dasarath gasped in shock.

A few minutes later, a shaking Dasarath stood outside an unmarked door and knocked. This time, there was no answer. He knocked again. When only silence greeted him, he turned the handle, pushed the door and entered the blackness.

At first, he saw nothing, but slowly, as his eyes became accustomed to the darkness he made out a figure laying on the floor. Dasarath rushed over, and knelt anxiously beside it.

"Kaikeyi! Kaikeyi, is that you? What has happened? Are you ill? My love, what is the matter? Kaikeyi, please, speak to me."

Kaikeyi made no reply, but turned her face away.

"Kaikeyi, my dearest," Dasarath cried, taking her in his arms and stroking her long hair. "Why don't you speak? Is it something I have done? Just tell me, please! Kaikeyi, I'll give you jewels, gold, pearls. Just name it! It shall be yours. I only want you to be happy. You know how much I love you. As monarch I have ultimate authority, I'll give you anything you desire. This I swear. Just, please say something!"

Kaikeyi looked straight up into Dasarath's eyes.

"My dear Kaikeyi, if it will only make you happy, I swear in the name of my dearest son, Ram, you can have anything you want."

Sure of victory, Kaikeyi smiled to herself, and rose, stretching out her arms to him. How it delighted her to see the undying love in Dasarath's eyes.

"Do you remember, my husband, on the battlefield long ago, when you were at death's door, pierced by arrows, your life force slipping away? I rescued you and drove you to safety, removed the arrows of death from your body, and nursed you back to health. When you recovered, you granted me two wishes to show your gratitude."

"Kaikeyi, I have never forgotten what you did for me during those terrible times. You were very brave. I will always be grateful to you."

"The wishes, Dasarath, the wishes."

"Yes, Kaikeyi, you still have them."

"You gave your word," asserted Kaikeyi, "I can ask for anything I want."

"Yes, anything, Kaikeyi. Anything."

Kaikeyi rose from the floor and whispered into his ear. Dasarath stiffened, and immediately slumped to the floor where his wife had lain, gripping his chest in pain as red-hot swords of shock racked through his body and the roar of storm tossed breakers pounded up the shore of his mind. Suddenly, he was back on the battlefield with the screams of the dying all around him, and arrows of death filling the air, piercing his body again and again, his consciousness passing in waves of light and dark.

"How can you ask this of me?" he dreamed, "What has Ram ever done to you?'

"You promised me, Dasarath. The boons are mine!"

"Sorceress!" he cried and knew no more until he woke to the sound of morning prayers. He opened his eyes and looked around, and found himself on the cold floor of the sulking room. Slowly, he recalled the events of the night before, and the pain started again.

He rose shakily, and then Kaikeyi entered his blurred vision, sitting at a table, running a brush through her long, dark hair.

"Tell Ram to come," she said. "The sooner he knows of his destiny, the better."

With great regret, Dasarath stretched his hand for the small bell and shook it. A moment later, a servant appeared.

"Send for Ram," he stammered.

CHAPTER 11

KAIKEYI'S AMBITION

As THE FIRST STREAKS of dawn appeared above the eastern horizon, prelude to a magnificent sunrise, Ayodhya teemed with activity as thousands of citizens put the final touches to the decorations, and vendors set up their stalls, ready for a surge of customers the day would bring.

Even at this early hour, townsfolk lined the streets all the way from Ram's apartments to the royal palace, chanting Ram's name over and over. Two citizens sat together outside the palace gates.

"It's going to be a wonderful day for the Coronation," said one elderly man.

"Yes," replied the other, "today will certainly go down in history."

At the front of Ram's mansion, resplendent with jeweled archways, sculptured figures and ornate carvings, Sumantra waited with a chariot. Ram appeared, boarded, and the chariot entered the street, horse's snorting, steaming the cold morning air with their breath, to be immediately surrounded by cheering, enthusiastic crowds.

"It's Prince Ram! All glories to Prince Ram!" they cried as he passed them. "Long live Prince Ram!"

Arriving at the palace, Ram went straight to Kaikeyi's chamber, finding her reclining on a velvet cushion, with Manthara close by. On the other side of the room, against the wall, near one of the long windows, slumped his father.

"Father! What's the matter?" Ram cried, as he spotted him. "Are you ill?"

"Your father is not ill," said Kaikeyi coldly, as Ram hurried to him. "He is about to fulfill a promise."

Ram looked into his father's mournful face.

"Father," he implored. "What is wrong?"

"My dear Ram," Kaikeyi purred, "there is nothing wrong with the king. His only infirmity is fear. Afraid to tell the truth. A king who is afraid is a king in a fool's body."

Ram was shocked to hear those words coming from Queen Kaikeyi, which were punctuated by Manthara's cackling laughter.

"Kaikeyi, please," begged Ram. "What is going on? It grieves me so much to see both of you like this."

"Oh Ram. Wise, just, noble Ram," she replied, pacing up and down. "You are so endearing. Let me tell you a story. When I was younger, I used to accompany the king to the battlefield. There I would watch as he valiantly fought the demonic forces of Ravan's army. But, once, during the night, Sambara, one of Ravan's warlords, led his rakshas warriors into our camp to attack the wounded as they slept. Dasarath responded, killing many, but sustained terrible wounds, and would have died had I not risked my own life in order to remove him to safety. In return, he granted me two wishes. I now desire those wishes to be fulfilled."

Ram looked at his father, and saw the truth confirmed in his eyes.

"What is it you want, Kaikeyi?" Ram said.

Relishing every moment, Kaikeyi took time to find the right words.

"For my first wish, I want Prince Bharat made king," she said. "And second, you are to be banished to the Dandaka forest for fourteen years!"

As Manthara hobbled about in an ecstatic dance, Ram felt those cruel words tear into Dasarath's heart. Brought up to uphold the highest ideals no matter what the circumstance, Prince Ramachandra paused thoughtfully before replying.

"I will not stand in Bharat's way," he said. "Nor am I attached to position, fame or riches, but follow the path of dharma, as befitting my position as a Royal Prince. If I could, for a moment, harbor any thoughts other than these, then I would pray to be delivered into the forest never to return. I have been taught to put no one into difficulty, either by word, thought or deed, nor to cause unnecessary suffering to any living being, so, Kaikeyi, if this is what you desire, then let it be so."

"You will leave for the forest immediately then!"

"No, Kaikeyi!" wailed Dasarath.

"Wear these," said Kaikeyi, thrusting clothing made from tree bark and deerskin, towards Ram.

Manthara, unable to hide her excitement, jumped up and down behind Kaikeyi as Ram took the garments.

"Ram, do not go alone," his father said. "Take a battalion of my men, and a chest from the treasury."

"No!" shouted Kaikeyi defiantly. "King Bharat will not accept an incomplete army or exchequer. Ram will leave Ayodhya alone. That is all, Ram. You may go."

The two men made a long embrace, and as Ram left the room, his father's loud lament followed him down the long, cold corridors, past the lavishly decorated throne room, from which he told himself, with heavy heart, he would never reign.

When Ram entered his mother's room, Kausalya, Sita and Lakshman greeted him.

"Ram, my son," Kausalya welcomed him, "We have just completed an all-night vigil for the Coronation. May your reign over Kosala be long and virtuous."

Ram went to his mother and placed his hands on her shoulders.

"Mother," he said, "there is something I must tell you. Father has just granted Kaikeyi two outstanding wishes."

"What does Kaikeyi want?"

"She wants Bharat to rule in my place."

"Impossible!" cried Lakshman.

"And her second wish?" asked Kausalya incredulously.

"I am exiled to the Dandaka for fourteen years."

"Oh, no!" sobbed his mother, falling into Ram's open arms.

"This is madness!" Lakshman shouted angrily, "Kaikeyi cannot do this!"

"Oh, Ram, what is going on?" Sita cried, bursting into tears.

"Mother, Sita, please do not upset yourselves," Ram said, "Bharat has noble qualities. He will make a righteous king."

"Ram, you are my son," said Kausalya shakily, hot tears streaming down her face. "You were to be king. Now all that is lost. Am I to lose you too?"

"Nowhere in our history has any member of our royal family been deprived of their rightful place on the throne," Lakshman declared, fighting back tears. "Ram, you are the eldest and therefore successor. No one can change that. Kaikeyi is the one who should be banished."

"Lakshman, we must follow the Vedic principles," Ram said quietly. "Our duty is to obey father. These are the codes set by the Rishis. We cannot go against them. I leave for the forest immediately."

As Ram turned to leave, Sita stretched out her hands, "No, Ram," she begged him. "You cannot go!"

"When Bharat is crowned," Ram said, grasping her hands, "serve him as you would me. Remember this. My love for you will never die."

"Ram, please take me with you," she cried, clinging to him. "My place is at your side. No one can keep us apart!"

"The Dandaka forest is no place for a woman, Sita," he explained, trying hard not to upset her. "It is full of wild beasts, snakes and thorny trees. The only food is what the forest provides, and sparsely at that. We drink from the stream and sleep under the stars. The noise from wild creatures is incessant. Your proper place is the palace, not the jungle. Ayodhya is your home. Wait for me here."

"Ram, you are my husband," cried Sita desperately. "Where you go, I go. We cannot be separated. If I stay here I will surely die."

"Sita, it is far too dangerous," he insisted.

"My husband, your duty is to protect me. How can you do that if you are away in the forest? If you go, there is no reason for me to stay here. Please take me with you."

As Sita fell into his arms, Ram melted. Easing her back, he looked deeply into her eyes. "Give your jewels and possessions to the Brahmins and the needy. Then prepare to leave."

"Brother, you have forgotten me," said Lakshman as Sita left the room.

"You must stay here and look after the queens," said Ram.

"But brother, you will need a servant. Who will guard you when you sleep? Who will search out food and scare away wild beasts?"

"Lakshman, it is I who is banished, not you."

"It is my sworn duty to serve you, brother. I cannot do that if you leave me here."

Ram thought a moment.

"Very well," he said, "bid farewell to Urmila, then go to the armory and bring our weapons. If the gods desire, we will all face the future together."

In Ram's apartments, Sita had tried dressing herself in the tree bark supplied by Kaikeyi, but found it almost impossible to wear it. Ram suggested she dress in a sari, and that he would attach the bark over the top. As Ram was fixing the bark in place, the door opened and a maidservant ushered Visvamitra into the room.

"Sita! Ram! What are you doing?" he asked.

"Gurudeva," replied Ram, "Sita must wear the tree bark before she leaves."

"No! I will not permit it. Sita will not wear tree bark. This I insist! She can wear a dress and some jewelry instead."

***

Lakshman said farewell to his mother, and received a lecture in return.

"Remember, Lakshman," Sumitra said solemnly, "Ram is your elder brother, and the future king. Do not neglect your duty. Serve and guard him, and show your devotion, at all times."

"I will never forget that Ram is my master," said Lakshman, "I will serve and love him always."

Ram and Lakshman, both dressed in the cloth of ascetics, wearing nothing more than tree bark and deerskin, were joined by Sita, dressed in a plain silken sari decorated with jewels, ready for the journey. For someone who was about to spend a lengthy stay in the forest, she looked beautiful, as radiant as a goddess.

Before leaving, Sita, Ram and Lakshman offered their respects to Dasarath, Kausalya and Sumitra, and after a tearful goodbye, made their way out through the palace doors where a chariot driven by Sumantra waited.

Word had quickly spread of Ram's imminent departure, and the citizens of Ayodhya, gathered on the streets and on balconies above the main thoroughfare, cried and wailed as they tried to stop the chariot from pulling away.

Further down the street a citizen shouted.

"Look! It's Prince Ram without an army. He's leaving without an army!"

At that, the entire street fell silent except for the clip clop of hooves striking stone. By the time they had reached the administrative buildings on the outer edge of the city; a crowd of weeping citizens, imploring them not to go, again surrounded their chariot.

Lakshman looked back at the palace, and saw Dasarath, leaning on a parapet, looking like an old man, his face full of grief, watching from a balcony. Behind him Sumitra and Kausalya stood, dabbing at their eyes. Dasarath swayed unsteadily, and was immediately supported by two aides.

As the carriage neared the city gate, Ram, wanting the pain of parting to be over quickly, turned to Sumantra and urged him on, and the carriage sped through the city gates.

From the balcony, Kausalya wept uncontrollably, as Dasarath watched the carriage until it had diminished to a speck. His eyes stayed fixed to the spot, hoping to catch one final glimpse, but it never came. He leaned over the balcony in despair.

How could this have happened, he asked himself. His own son, successor to the throne of Ayodhya banished to the forest. How degrading. How unthinkable. With these thoughts weighing heavily on his mind, the King suddenly collapsed, and was quickly removed by attendants, followed anxiously by Sumitra.

As Kausalya followed through the doorway, she turned for one final look.

The King groaned, and fell, sobbing and muttering, onto the cushions where Kausalya and Sumitra joined him.

"Kaikeyi has committed a great blunder," cried Dasarath. "Whatever possessed her? She does not deserve to be my wife. Bharat would never, for one moment, consider taking the throne from his brother. If she thought this, then all she has learnt in her lifetime is worth nothing. I do not want to see her again."

Kausalya stroked Dasarath's forehead, thinking that Ram could not have asked for more devoted companions, and that, one day, he would return and rule the kingdom.

As soon as Dasarath was calmer, Kausalya helped him to his bed where he lay, sobbing and pouring out his grief.

CHAPTER 12

BANISHMENT

SUMANTRA DROVE THE CARRIAGE south at a steady pace, into the vast expanse of open, barren countryside, Ayodhya gradually fading into the distance behind them. As Sita, Ram and Lakshman traveled along the dusty road, a broad belt of trees came ever nearer until it filled the entire horizon, forming an unbroken barrier before them. A feeling of foreboding entered their hearts as they moved, irrevocably, towards it.

Although, from a distance, the Dandaka looked like an inviting, peaceful and serene place, some of those who were lured there soon realized they had put themselves in danger, and felt a very unwelcome vibration.

The thought of spending the next fourteen years in the forest gave them all much to think about.

"Is it safe there, Ram?" Sita asked as they neared the first wall of trees.

"Don't worry Sita, Lakshman and I will take very good care of you," he assured her.

Replete as it was with many different species of plants, beautiful flowers, shrubs, trees, rivers and lakes, the Dandaka forest was an enticing haven, but some unfortunate travelers, wandering into the forest by accident, captivated by its primal beauty, soon lost themselves among the labyrinth of paths, and unaware of the dangers within, were never seen again.

Occasionally, screams were heard within the forest's unfathomable depths, until silence descended, entombing all within.

There were many tales of the Dandaka, some incredible, many barely believable. Most sane travelers preferred to avoid the strange world of the giant trees with its carnivorous man-eating plants, and the unfamiliar wild animals that roamed its interior.

It was also home to the sub-human rakshas.

***

The sun was setting when Sita, Ram and Lakshman traveled down a trail that led them to a clearing beside a wide river. There they saw a landing stage where a small boat was tied up, and through the mist, on the far side, lay the Dandaka Forest.

Deciding to set up camp beside the river, Ram helped Sita prepare to bed down near the carriage while Lakshman and Sumantra took care of the horses. As Sita and Ram slept, Lakshman and Sumantra took turns keeping watch. Just after sun up the next day, they prepared to move on.

"This is where we must part company, Sumantra," said Ram, taking his friend by the shoulder.

"It's been a pleasure serving you, my Lord. Please take good care of yourself, and Sita."

"God bless you, Sumantra."

Once the trio had boarded, the boatman cast off without a word, and they drifted off down the wide river, not knowing what awaited them round the next bend.

By early afternoon, after they had traveled many miles, the boat having been beached on a sandbar, they disembarked and headed into the forest, accompanied by the sounds of crickets and clicking beetles, leaving behind them the last traces of civilization, knowing that, from here on in, there would be only wilderness. Ram and Lakshman, according to an age-old custom attributed to mendicants, wore their hair in matted locks.

They had been walking for an hour along a damp trail through dense undergrowth, when Sita stopped to listen.

"Something is moving out there," she said.

"It could be an animal or a rakshas demon," suggested Lakshman.

"Lakshman, don't go frightening Sita like that," said Ram, breaking off as a strange cry split the air.

"Ram, I don't like this," said Sita.

"What was that?" whispered Lakshman.

"Whatever it was, it won't stand much chance against our weapons."

They both looked around, trying to locate the sound.

"Come on," said Ram, as they continued along the trail, deeper into the forest, "It's just some harmless creature."

Behind them a vine slithered out of the brush, wrapped itself around a small rabbit, and dragged it, struggling, into the undergrowth.

The first few days in the forest were an uncomfortable experience for everyone, especially Sita. Although she missed the comforts of the palace, Sita soon became accustomed to spending the nights in the open.

As the end of another day arrived, they again looked for a more suitable place to spend the night, and settled on a sheltered hollow where Sita soon fell asleep on the bed Ram prepared for her out of fallen leaves.

"Brother, I don't think Sita should have come with us," said Lakshman when he returned from gathering firewood. "The forest is no place for a Princess."

"Sita is brave and steadfast," Ram told him. "Surely you have noticed she has voiced no complaint."

"Yes, but will she be able to put up with the hardship of forest life for the many years to come," his brother grumbled. "That's what worries me."

"Only time will tell," Ram replied. "Tomorrow we look for the hermitage of Sage Bharadvaja. He should know of a place we can stay."

"Ram, I wonder what's happening in Ayodhya?"

"It's best we forget Ayodhya, brother."

"Forget Ayodhya?"

"Yes, brother, difficult as it is bound to be, we must forget."

CHAPTER 13

DASARATH

THE STRESS OF RAM'S banishment had aged King
Dasarath considerably, and for three days he took to
his couch, where he lay all day rocking back and forth,
sometimes groaning aloud, sometimes crying like a
child, lamenting the loss of his sons, nursed by Kausalya
with warm caring devotion. With each passing day he
became more morose, refusing food or any kind of
sustenance. For long periods at a time he would remain
silent, staring off into space, chanting Ram's name as if
that was the only thing left to do in the world.

Kausalya tried in vain to comfort him, but knew
she could only do so much. So great was Dasarath's
love for Ram, that there was little she could say to
lift the crippling burden of grief. Each day since that
fateful hour of Ram's untimely departure, Dasarath
became more grief stricken, and the thought of not
seeing his favorite son for many years eroded away his
will to live.

At first light on the morning of the seventh day after Ram's departure, a maid entered Dasarath's apartment, and found him dead. Her screams brought Kausalya and Sumitra running. Kausalya lightly touched the dead King's face and sat down, placing Dasarath's head on her lap.

"My dear, dear husband," she said sadly, "you died of a broken heart. May you now find peace."

"How could Kaikeyi have been so cruel?" cried Sumitra.

The sad news spread all over Ayodhya, and the city went into deep mourning. Now that the King was dead, they needed to find Bharat, and quickly. Vasishtha issued an immediate proclamation ordering a meeting in the Council Hall.

"Markendeya and the Brahmins suggest we send for Bharat and Shatrughna," announced Kausalya. "They have to be told."

"Yes," Vasishtha agreed, "Without a ruler we leave ourselves open to attack. Bharat and Shatrughna should return as soon as possible, but it would be prudent not to give them the bad news till their arrival." And calling a messenger. "Go to Kekaya. Tell Bharat and Shatrughna they must return immediately."

***

In the Dandaka forest, Sita, Ram and Lakshman walked along a high ridge, climbing steadily towards a range of majestic hills where, reaching a wooded plateau, they sat down to rest. It was Ram who spotted a plume of smoke in the distance.

"Lakshman! A campfire," he exclaimed. "That must be the ashram of Bharadvaja."

"He must be an austere sage living so isolated from his fellow man," said Sita.

"At least he is far from the problems of civilization," Lakshman noted as they rose to continue their travels.

Bharadvaja's ashram was tucked away in a hidden corner of the woods, and as they approached, the elderly ascetic appeared, accompanied by two monks.

"Please accept my respects, master," Ram said, introducing himself. This is my wife Sita and my brother Lakshman."

"It is an honor, Ram," the sage replied. I am Bharadvaja. Welcome to my abode. Please come sit and rest."

"Thank you. We'll be in the Dandaka for some time, and are looking for a place to stay."

"You have been through many trials, Ram," the sage replied, "but look no further. My ashram is simple but it will meet your needs."

"Thank you for your kind offer, Bharadvaja, but this is too close to Ayodhya. If the citizens know we are here, they will come to beseech us to return. We need to find somewhere more distant."

"I know of a place in the Chitrakuta Mountains, two or three day's travel from here," the sage mused. "It is an elevated retreat surrounded by lakes and forests, and magnificent scenery. No one ever goes there."

"That sounds perfect," said Ram.

Early next day, Ram, Sita and Lakshman left Bharadvaja with hope in their hearts, and headed towards the mountains in the distance.

CHAPTER 14

RETURN OF THE BROTHERS

A WEEK LATER, BHARAT and Shatrughna arrived back in Kosala. As they entered Ayodhya's main gate, they were surprised to find no signs of the usual city activity, no music being played in the main square, and no garlands hanging from balconies. In fact, the city looked dead and deserted.

"Strange," Shatrughna said, "there's no one about."

"I wonder why they sent for us?" Bharat said, perplexed.

Thundering up to the palace, past subdued guards, they saw Kaikeyi and Manthara on the palace steps.

Bharat quickly dismounted and ran to embrace his mother.

"Bharat! Shatrughna, welcome back," Kaikeyi said. "It's good to see you again. You must be very tired from your long journey."

"We were ordered to return immediately," Bharat said. "What has happened here? The whole city seems to be in mourning. Where is father? Why isn't he here to greet us?"

"Your father had not been well lately."

"What!" Bharat cried, breaking his mother's embrace. "Where is he?"

Kaikeyi grabbed his arm, but Bharat broke free and ran into the palace, calling for his father.

"Wait!" she cried, racing after him.

Bharat went straight to his father's chambers, and finding it empty, rushed into the corridor, bumping into Kaikeyi.

"Bharat! We have to talk," Kaikeyi said.

"Where's father?" Bharat demanded, his voice thick with emotion. "What's going on around here? Where is everyone?"

"Please calm down, my son," Kaikeyi begged him, "I have some bad news. Your father, my husband, our king, has passed from this mortal world."

"Nooooooo!" he cried, falling back against the wall, mind failing to function.

The young prince wailed incoherently, tears streaming down his face, then turned to the wall, pounding it with his fists.

"I am so sorry, my son," Kaikeyi told him. "But your father took to his bed and a decline set in which the physician could not halt."

"Where is Ram?" Bharat sobbed, trying to recover. "Where's Sita? Lakshman? Where is everyone?"

"Ram has gone."

"What! Ram gone? Gone where?" Bharat cried incredulously.

"To find his destiny!" she told him. "You see, your father decided on a successor and choose Ram. I objected to this and…"

"What?" Bharat croaked. "You did what?"

"Bharat, please understand. I wanted you to be king."

"Mother, this is unheard of. I, I can't believe…"

"I was owed a boon for saving your father's life!"

"I don't believe what you're saying!"

"Bharat, you're my son! I did this for you!"

"No, mother, no! This is impossible. Where is Ram?"

"Don't worry, Bharat," said Kaikeyi, "Ram's banishment is only fourteen years…"

"Ram, banished?"

"Yes. But everything will be all right. Sita and Lakshman are with him in the Dandaka…"

"The Dandaka! Sita! Fourteen years in the Dandaka? Don't you know the whole place is full of rakshas? What have you done?"

"It was Manthara! She told me to ask for the boons I was owed…"

"Manthara! You listened to her?"

"Bharat, I only desired you to be king. It was Manthara who wanted to banish Ram!"

"You have committed a great offense against our family and have brought shame upon the Solar Dynasty! And I know exactly what to do with Manthara!" he said grimly on seeing the old woman approach.

"Your father died a few days after they left," Kaikeyi sobbed, dabbing her eyes. "He was so devoted to Ram. But all your worries are over now, my son. The crown and the kingdom are yours."

"Am I dreaming this?" Bharat demanded, glaring at his mother. "Will I wake up and find myself with Ram, Sita and my brothers again? I cannot believe that you allowed this reptile to implicate me in her web of evil. How could you even contemplate such a thing?"

"I did it for you, Bharat!"

"This is madness. What makes you think I could be a part of this? That... that I could sit on the throne of Ayodhya and rule as if nothing had happened, while Sita, Ram and Lakshman risk their lives in the Dandaka? If you believe this of me, then you are no longer my mother."

Bharat strode off, and then spun.

"I will not rest until Ram returns and takes his rightful place on the throne of Ayodhya!"

And with that, Bharat ran down the hallway, shouting Ram's name at the top of his voice as Kaikeyi sank to the floor, sobbing uncontrollably.

***

As the full Council of ministers, Brahmins and royal advisors assembled in the Council Hall to discuss the matter, Bharat arrived and went to Vasishtha.

"I have disowned my mother," he declared. "I will never forgive her."

"But Bharat, you must take the throne, Vasishtha told him, "It was your father's final request."

"I will not rule a kingdom obtained through deceit," replied Bharat, jumping onto a table and raising both arms. "Listen to me, all of you! The throne of Ayodhya belongs to Ram. It is his by birthright. This is the law of the land and I will uphold it until my dying breath."

At that moment Kaikeyi entered the room, standing at the back with her face covered.

"Kaikeyi is to blame for all this," Bharat shouted vehemently, pointing at her scornfully. "She has piled misery onto everyone in Ayodhya. Now it's up to me to right this wrong. I am going after Ram."

Bharat jumped down and shouted to a Minister.

"Kashyapa, order the generals to ready a battalion! Two weeks rations! We leave at once!"

"But Bharat, how do we find Ram?" Shatrughna said as they pushed their way toward the door. "The Dandaka is immense."

"God is on our side."

CHAPTER 15

IN SEARCH OF RAM

At first light the next day, Bharat, Shatrughna, Sumantra, and a detachment of soldiers, leaving a long cloud of dust hanging in the air, rode out of Ayodhya. After three days of hard travel and diligent searching, they arrived at the ashram of Bharadvaja, who informed them of Ram's departure in the direction of Chitrakuta. By early evening Bharat ordered a halt.

"Ram is somewhere in this area," he announced. "I can feel it. We will camp here tonight."

By late afternoon of the next day, when they had progressed even deeper into the forest, Bharat could feel Ram's presence more strongly, and sent out a scout, who returned shortly afterwards with good news, saying, "There is a campfire up ahead, Prince Bharat."

Bharat turned to Sumantra.

"That has to be Ram!" he cried. "Stay here with half the detachment. Shatrughna, you and your men follow me."

It was dusk by the time they reached the campsite, where smoke from the fire drifted lazily up through the trees.

Bharat was excited, yet confused as he slowly picked his way through the brush. He saw the golden bows leaning against a tree, but there was no sign of Ram or Lakshman. Then Shatrughna saw them sleeping in the shadows beyond the fire. Before they could speak, the ever-vigilant Ram sprang to his feet and called out, "Who's there?" And then seeing his brother opened his arms and embraced him tightly, as Sita awoke.

"Ram," Bharat exclaimed. "Thank goodness I've found you. Brother, you must return to Ayodhya. Without a ruler, our country is like a ship without a captain, and will surely flounder."

"Slow down, brother," Ram replied. "What are these strange words I hear? What has happened in Ayodhya? How is father?"

Bharat took a deep breath.

"Ram, after you left for the forest, our grieving father gave up his body," he said.

"Oh, father," Ram cried, as Sita embraced him.

"Kausalya said he died of a broken heart," Bharat continued.

"Oh father, I will never hear your voice again."

"Please, brother, return to Ayodhya and take your rightful place on the throne," Bharat begged him, starting to cry. "There is no one to rule over Kosala. The people need you."

"Bharat, I know it's hard for you at this time," Ram said, recovering, "but the first lesson we learn as *ksatriyas*, and as human beings, is to honor and obey our father and mother. It is the duty of everyone. If we do not, the world would not be a fit place in which to live. It was father's wish that I be sent to the forest. Whether I like it or not, it is my dharma, it is my life."

"Brother, your rightful place is on the throne of Ayodhya," Bharat protested, "not wandering this wretched forest. You are the eldest, and the next in line. By virtue of evil trickery, I have found myself named king, even though I am not qualified to rule. I can never hope to imitate you Ram, and you are the guiding light of my life, therefore take up your proper duty and return..."

"But, Bharat..."

"If you refuse, I will fast unto death. I cannot bear this torment a moment longer."

"I understand how you feel, brother," Ram replied, "but this is not the conduct of a ksatriya. This material world is a sea of suffering. As long as there is birth and death, there will be old age, disease and hardship. The rising and setting of the sun decreases the duration of life for everyone, except those who inquire about the Absolute Truth. We are simply actors on the stage of life, continually suffering in a never-ending tragedy. We should contemplate this and accept the Vedic conclusions on *karma* as best we can. This is the creed of our father, and all the Acaryas in our line. Therefore my brother, return to Ayodhya, and take care of the kingdom, it is your duty, as much as it is mine to remain here."

"No, Ram," Bharat told him earnestly. "The kingdom is rightfully yours. I cannot rule in your place."

"Ram, if you will not return, then let something of yours represent you on the throne," Shatrughna suggested."

"I will agree to that," Ram said, slipping off his sandals and handing them to Bharat, who, before taking them, prostrated himself at Ram's feet.

"Ram," said Bharat, "I will place these sandals on the throne of Ayodhya, and they will govern in your place. I shall live outside Ayodhya until your return."

"I accept. But to please me further, brother, do not think badly of Kaikeyi. Though she may have done unworthy things, she is still your mother. Do not be angry with her."

Ram, Lakshman and Bharat embraced, then Bharat turned to go.

"May you be blessed, Bharat," said Ram, as he watched them ride off into the night.

The next day, Ram tried to put all that had happened, to the back of his mind. The compassion he felt for his younger brother, and the burden of his own banishment strengthened him, giving him the courage and stamina he knew he would need to face the Dandaka.

That evening, while they sat around the campfire, Ram, who had given much thought to the matter, suddenly spoke. "Lakshman, we must leave Chitrakuta."

"Leave Chitrakuta?"

"We must move on."

***

Bharat and Shatrughna arrived back in Ayodhya, and went directly to the throne room. Pushing open the door, its squeaking hinges echoed through the cavernous palace, admitting a sharp rectangle of sunlight that exposed the drabness of a place that had lost its former luster.

"Long may you reign, dear brother," Bharat said, bowing to place Ram's sandals at the base of the throne. Then facing Shatrughna. "Ayodhya is no longer a place of joy, brother. The whole city is in mourning. Let us depart for Nandigram."

As they left, the heavy creaking door slammed deafeningly behind them, as if signifying the end of an era, stirring up a draft of stale air that wafted through the expansive room, dislodging layers of dust that churned slowly through the dankness, highlighted by the afternoon sunlight.

Outside, weeds growing in the deserted courtyard rocked in the breeze, debris blew along the deserted streets, and a lonely citizen trudged homeward under a leaden sky.

CHAPTER 16

DEEP IN THE FOREST

IN ANCIENT TIMES, THOSE with spiritual inclinations
and a desire to practice the art of meditation left for
the seclusion and solitude of the remoter parts of the
earth. The forests and high mountain ranges of the
Himalayas, destinations of many sages intent on
detaching themselves from the material world in order
to attain understanding of the Absolute Truth, provided
the ideal environment. Their sheer inaccessibility
guaranteed isolation from the ever-active influence of
rampant materialism that constantly exerted its grip
on the living entity.

For those aspiring ascetics, the higher world
offered more, a freeing of the consciousness, the pure
light of eternal life, and a chance to experience the
nearness of God.

The Dandaka forest, like similar jungles, also
attracted the spiritual seeker, just as much as that of
the distant isolated mountains.

The Dandaka, traditionally a place for monks and sages to meditate, contained many ashrams, meager lodgings, often no more than a few sticks supporting a roof of leaves, from which their few belongings hung. Devoid of all material possessions, these mendicants were then free to concentrate their focus of attention on the Divine, and achieve a higher state of being.

As Ram, Sita and Lakshman made their way along the dim, winding forest trails, they came across many of these spiritual oases.

The sound of Vedic mantras, part of the forest symphony, wafted through the green leafy glades, uplifting the many mendicants who decided to spent time in this green world where sweet scented flowers grew along the grassy banks and beside the forest trails, and delicate creepers wove themselves through the tangle of random flora, while countless birds filled the air with their song.

Its beauty and abundant life, a certain sign of a caring Creator, moved Sita, Ram, and Lakshman. However, as they continued to penetrate deeper into the jungle, the forest began to take on an eerie countenance.

Ram noticed the change of atmosphere, one that became heavier with each passing day. The animals more dangerous, and primitive, the flora more primordial, including in their number, the vicious, black, man-eating lilies and giant flytrap orchids, in which lay the rotting remains of long dead creatures.

Strange trees populated the landscape, and the sweet songs of the colorful birds gradually gave way to a lasting silence that penetrated everywhere, as if pre-warning an impending disaster.

"Ram, am I imagining things, or are these trees getting taller?" Lakshman said uneasily.

"I noticed that a while ago," Ram agreed. "We seem to have entered a rather strange part of the forest."

"I feel something terrible is going to happen," whispered Lakshman.

They moved on, but Sita lagged behind, attracted by the weird splendor of the forest plants.

***

The trio wandered the Dandaka forest for many years, visiting various ashrams, getting to know the holy men before moving on again. Sometimes they remained for a month or two, but always moving on, like the nomads they had become.

Nor did they find peace. Rakshas attacked, sometimes without warning, leaving them exhausted and edgy, but after what seemed an eternity, the attacks stopped, signaling that, at last, they had left rakshas territory behind.

One day, the noble Sita, who from the very beginning of their exile had resigned herself to take her share of the burden of banishment on her slim shoulders, felt she could bear it no longer.

Womanlike, she had a strong natural yearning for a permanent home, a place where she could spend the rest of her years until the time came for them to return to Ayodhya, a yearning that at last became so heavy within her that she sat down on a bank and cried.

"Ram, for years we've been walking through this forest, which seems to have no end," she sobbed when he came to her. "Why can't we find somewhere and build a home, settle down and be happy?"

"Sita is right," Lakshman said, "As far as we know, we could have left rakshas country far behind, and somewhere nearby could be a good place to build a home."

Ever since they left Ayodhya, these thoughts had always been in the forefront of Ram's mind. During their epic stay in the Dandaka, he had been occupied with many worries - now, as a devoted husband who dearly loved his wife, he realized that he must put her interests and safety first.

"All right, Lakshman," he said. "Tomorrow we will look for a suitable place to stay."

As he finished speaking, a haunting cry rang out through the forest, sending chills right through Lakshman.

CHAPTER 17

SAGE AGASTYA

DAYLIGHT FADED ONCE MORE, as they trudged, tired and sleepy, through the forest, stopping only when Sita stumbled and fell. As Ram hastened to help her to her feet, dark clouds scudded across the face of the moon, strange sounds reverberated through the forest, and a sudden breeze rustled the leaves. It was then that they saw the light.

As they approached, a man of small stature, with distinctive red and white markings on his forehead, came out of a small grass hut to meet them. He bowed to Ram.

"Welcome to our ashram, my friends," he said. "My name is *Agastya*."

"This is an honor," Ram said, offering his obeisances. "I've heard a great deal about you. I am Prince Ram of Ayodhya. This is my wife Sita, and my brother Lakshman."

"Come, please make yourselves comfortable," said Agastya, ushering them across to a small fire, to where he had prepared a meal.

"You look tired," he said, sympathetically, signaling a monk in orange robes to bring food and drink.

"We have been wandering the Dandaka forest for many years," Ram told him, "spending a day or two at various ashrams, or simply sleeping under the stars, before moving on. But now, we just want to find a permanent place to live."

"The forest we have gone through was full of rakshas demons," Lakshman said, "Is it safe here?"

"We are quite safe," Agastya assured him, "For some time now, we have felt your guardian presence. Vasishtha has taught you well, Ram."

After they had eaten, Agastya disappeared into the forest, returning shortly afterwards with two aides. Each carried a large bundle wrapped in luxurious purple cloth.

"The sages and holy ones of the forest value your protection, Ram. In return, they offer you these gifts."

The monks unwrapped the bundles, and revealed two bows, two quivers, two swords and suits of armor. Agastya picked up the larger bow, constructed with three beautiful bends, and inlaid with gold and precious stones.

"This bow was designed by Vishvakarma and used by Lord *Narayan* Himself to fight the *asuras* during the Great War of the Heavens," Agastya explained. "Its power is infinite. An inexhaustible quiver of arrows, and a sword completes the set. There is also a special suit of armor, which cannot be pierced, courtesy of

Lord *Indra*. But, be warned, these weapons possess great mystical potency. Use them wisely."

"Thank you, Agastya," Ram said as the sage handed him the bow. "This is indeed exquisite."

"This is an amazing bow," Lakshman exclaimed admiringly.

"These are divine weapons, Ram," Agastya said. "If you are ever called upon to use them, make sure it is only to uphold the highest ideal."

Agastya removed a crescent shaped arrow from its special compartment in the quiver.

"This is the Brahmastra, equal in power to ten thousand suns. Use it only as a last resort. Once fired, it cannot be recalled. Choose your target well."

"These are the mantras you will need to invoke the astras," Agastya went on, passing a roll of parchment to Ram. "Memorize them."

Lakshman picked up a sword, and weighed it carefully in his hand. The silver scabbard, set with precious stones, gleamed in the firelight.

"We must be careful these weapons don't fall into the wrong hands, brother," he said.

Ram pulled on the bowstring, feeling its power. Hearing the bow tingling, the monks stopped what they were doing and looked up, and Sita marveled, remembering the day she had first seen Ram, the day he had won her hand.

Agastya took Ram to one side.

"Ram, Sita is very special, and also very tender. Coming to the forest, giving up a much easier life in the palace, she has demonstrated her love and devotion for you. Many would balk at entering a life of such austerity and hardship, but Sita put her personal comfort last. She has truly divine qualities, and will always be faithful and true. Because of her, your wanderings in the Dandaka are at an end, Ram. The place you are looking for is not far from here. You will find it after four days. It's a very beautiful place. They call it Panchavati. You will be happy there. The forest will provide you with food, fuel, materials to build a hut, and a plentiful supply of fruit and fresh water. It will be very much like paradise."

"May you be blessed, Agastya!" Ram replied gratefully.

The next morning, Agastya showed them a path into the forest.

"Go south along this trail until you come to a large hill," he said. "On the far side, you will find a small meadow beside a stream. That is your destination."

Sita, Ram and Lakshman offered their respects to sage Agastya, and with renewed vigor, set off in search of Panchavati.

CHAPTER 18

TO PANCHAVATI

THE NEXT DAY, AS they passed near some exceptionally tall forest, singing, and laughing, they heard a noise coming from a nearby eucalyptus tree.

"Ram! Listen. There's something up there," cried Sita.

"Are you hearing things again, Sita," Lakshman teased her.

"This time it's for real!" she insisted. "Listen. The leaves of that tree are rustling."

"Sita, stand well back," Ram ordered, then drew his sword as a dark shadow fell on them. "Lakshman! Move over there."

"By the gods! It's a demon!" Lakshman shouted, drawing his sword as a giant eagle swooped down landing near them. Sita hid behind Ram, covering her face.

The two princes stood poised to strike, but the eagle calmly folded its wings and squawked, "Greetings, forest dwellers."

"Who are you? What do you want?" Ram demanded.

"Do not be alarmed," the bird replied. "I wish you no harm. I am a friend. My name is Jatayu, brother of Sampati. I have been sent to guide and protect you during your stay in the forest. Our father is Aruna, brother of Garuda, bird carrier of Lord Vishnu. I am just an old eagle who has seen better days."

"Oh, Ram, isn't he sweet," said Sita, venturing out from behind her husband, who sheathed his sword and then introduced them.

"It's a pleasure to meet you," Jatayu said. "We are not too far from Panchavati, you know."

"How did you know about Panchavati?" Lakshman asked.

"Apparently, there are no secrets in the forest, Lakshman," Ram said.

"If you follow me, I will guide you," squawked Jatayu, pointing with his wing. "Panchavati lies in that direction. Or is it that direction? This forest is so big, I sometimes get a little confused."

"Ram, I don't believe this is happening," Sita said laughing.

"All right, Jatayu," said Ram, clearly amused. "You lead, we'll follow."

"Stand well back, then."

Flapping his wings, Jatayu took off, creating a gale force wind that nearly knocked them off their feet.

"I'm glad he's a friend," Ram said grinning.

They continued on their journey, happier now that someone was looking out for them. But it was not long before a small incident occurred, which tore, with unexpected ferocity, at Ram's heart.

Throughout all the time since that fateful day when Ram was banished, Sita had endured the hardships that came with living under a roof of stars, without complaint simply because of her undying love for her husband.

During the afternoon of the third day after meeting Jatayu, however, she was so tired that she lay down on a dry patch of ground.

"Ram," she cried, as Ram bent down beside her. "Why can't we stop here? I can't go on."

"It's only a little further, Sita."

"I am so exhausted. It's been such a long time since I've slept under a roof," Sita cried, distressing Ram with her words.

"Sita I promise you that we've nearly reached our destination. Please, just a little longer. We have Jatayu guiding us. We're nearly at Panchavati."

Ram helped Sita to her feet, and she leaned against him, supported by his arm, as they walked on. Then Lakshman spotted Jatayu circling above. He was pointing with his wing tip.

"Ram," he cried, "Jatayu is pointing to something!"

They followed, and the deep forest gradually opened out into a clearing, filled with dappled sunlight. Further on, they passed through a grassy plain, and in the distance, they saw a large hill, just as Agastya described it. As Ram helped Sita, Lakshman went in front and reached the summit first.

As Ram and Sita crested the hill, a spectacular scene met their eyes. Spread out below them was

Panchavati, the valley of their dreams, a lovely meadow lying snugly beside a winding stream, surrounded by fruit trees and flowering shrubs.

Sita was enchanted, her fatigue forgotten.

"Ram, what a wonderful place."

"Paradise," quipped Lakshman.

"Panchavati," said Ram.

"Oh, Ram, can we really call this place home?"

"Yes Sita, this is home. Lakshman, let's find the best place for our hut."

Flocks of brilliantly colored birds flew overhead as they descended the gentle slope.

"Look, Ram. Flamingoes, and peacocks!" Sita cried.

They ran through the lush ankle deep grass towards the stream, Sita picking flowers as they went.

"This place has been designated by the gods," Ram declared.

Ram soon found the perfect spot, close to the river on level ground, surrounded by kadamba trees, the air full with the perfume of lotus blossoms and wild flowers, accompanied by the tuneful ripple of a small stream. Birds chirped from the bushes, while peacocks sang songs of love.

It was the perfect setting.

"We'll build the hut right here," Ram said, as he marked the ground. "Its so peaceful that I feel we could live happily here forever."

Sita stood beside Ram with a freshly picked bunch of flowers, offering them to him before smelling them herself.

"Mmmm, listen to the birds," she murmured.

"Yes," Ram said, taking it all in. But even as he began to make plans to settle, his mind raced ahead. He knew total happiness did not last forever.

CHAPTER 19

THE COTTAGE

THE FIRST NIGHT, SITA was so excited she could hardly sleep, staying up late talking to Ram about their future in Panchavati. Now, she could be a real housewife, carrying out her wifely chores, cooking, cleaning and looking after the house.

"Ram," she whispered.

"Mmmm."

"I can't wait to cook for you. There are so many woodland recipes I want to try out."

"And I love eating what you offer me, Sita."

"I can't imagine how happy we'll be. I will be safe, won't I, Ram?"

"Yes, Sita. When you're with me, you'll be perfectly safe. Also, Lakshman will protect you when I'm away, and there is Jatayu. He's a good watchman. Just be happy."

"Yes… I shall… be… very… happy." Sita's words trailed off as she fell asleep.

Before the sun was up, Ram had completed his bath, and was sitting, quietly performing his morning worship. Lakshman, who has risen later, returned with an armful of wood, and proceeded to light the fire. After completing his prayers, Ram joined him to discuss the construction of the cottage. Lakshman could start on the building work while they are away picking fruit and berries in the valley. He had already scouted the surrounding area in search of wood, so knew what was available. Vines, palm leaves, bamboo and bark, it was all there.

By the end of the first day, the sides were up, together with a doorway and one window. A few days later Lakshman had completed the walls and was well ahead with the roof. This was the most difficult part, as it had to be watertight since, in this part of the forest, it could rain quite heavily.

On the third day, by the time Ram and Sita returned from the forest, the hut was finished.

"Lakshman, this is fantastic!" exclaimed Ram, embracing his brother. "How did you build it so fast?"

"I built it with love and devotion," Lakshman replied to the sound of their laughter.

That evening, before moving in, Ram performed a ceremony to bless the little cottage, and prayed to Lord Vishnu for protection.

As the days turned into weeks, and then months, Panchavati turned into the utopia they had dreamt of since leaving Ayodhya all those years ago. Every day brought a different kind of bliss into their lives, and there was so much to do in paradise.

But, one morning, while Sita sat outside the cottage stringing a garland of flowers, she shed a tear.

"Oh, Ram, I miss my family," she said in a melancholy voice. "Although I would rather be here with you, than in Ayodhya without you."

"Be strong, Sita," Ram replied, placed a garland of flowers over Sita's head as Lakshman handed her some fruit. "I know it's natural for you to feel like this, but we should try to maintain evenness of mind amid pleasant and unpleasant events. It will help us."

That evening, as they sat by the dying fire, Sita leaning against Ram, they looked up at the sky. The night air was filled with the smell of the forest, of musk and fir, and the aroma of herbs and spices, as insects clicked in the background and a billion stars twinkled brightly overhead.

"Oh, Ram. What a wonderful sight," said Sita. "It makes me feel so insignificant. Is the universe as old as they say?"

"Older."

"How old?"

"Older than any of us can imagine."

"Where did it all come from?"

"From the Supreme Personality of Godhead, the Source of Souls," he told her. "Creator of both the material and spiritual worlds."

"But where did the Supreme Personality of Godhead come from?"

"He's always existed, Sita. There wasn't a time when He did not exist, and we are all His parts and parcels, eternal and blissful. But the presence of the three modes of material nature makes life an ongoing struggle on all the planets in the universe," he continued. "Resulting in birth and death, heat, cold, happiness and distress, pleasure and pain. We are entrapped here by the temporary material energy, Sita, which is very strong and difficult to overcome, but, by practice, we can pass beyond it. Everyone has free will to accept or reject that. But those who choose to follow the spiritual path can cross beyond, and gain liberation from the cycle of birth, death, old age and disease. Far in the future, in the Age of Kali, the generations populating this planet will experience very heavy karma. There will be wars, new diseases, famine, animal killing and illness of the mind."

"I know I made the right choice being with you, Ram," Sita said lovingly, looking up at him with large lotus eyes.

Ram took Sita's hand and gazed back.

"I know I have, too," he replied.

In the night sky, the Milky Way glowed like a pale scarf stretched across the heavenly vault, and the world was at peace, safe in the arms of the night.

CHAPTER 20

SHURPANAK

ONE MORNING, A FEW days later, after collecting water from the stream, Ram returned to the cottage as usual, carrying a full pot, and placed it on the bamboo table Lakshman had made. Picking up his bow, he pulled on the string a few times, and then stiffened.

Ram felt someone, somewhere, was watching him.

He could feel their prying eyes marking his every move. After scanning the tree line, two hundred yards away, he threw a quiver full of arrows across his shoulder and strapped on his sword.

Many times in the past, rakshas had lain in wait for them, attacking without warning. A few times they had caught Ram alone, but he had always managed to deal with them.

A bird flew up out of the nearby bush.

"Yes, right there," Ram muttered to himself.

Concealed behind a large bush a short distance away, crouched Shurpanak, a rakshas demoness of short stature, with pig-like face, potbelly, wild coppery hair, and long sharp nails. From the moment she had set eyes on Ram, she to wanted to possess him. Gurgling and hissing behind the bush, she gazed at him with her red, watery eyes, the beauty of his masculine form instilling in her a lustful thirst, which she found unable to quench.

Now, realizing that she had been spotted, Shurpanak stepped into the open, and saw Ram staring at her in disbelief. She slowly made her way towards the cottage.

As she approached, Ram rested a hand on his sword handle.

"O lotus-eyed one," said Shurpanak, "you are a stranger to these parts, and, I might add, a very handsome one at that. You dress like a rishi, yet carry arms. This is rakshas country. It can be very dangerous for such a perfectly formed man. Tell me, who are you, and what are you doing in this, inhospitable part of the forest?"

"My dear lady," replied Ram, unperturbed, "I'm Prince Ram of Ayodhya, eldest son of King Dasarath of the Ishvakus. I am here performing *tapasya* in the forest. Pray, who are you?"

Lakshman returned from his walk with an armful of fruit, which he nearly dropped when he saw Shurpanak. He gazed at her in horror as he slowly placed the fruit on the table.

"I am Shurpanak, sister to the heroic Ravan, King of the Rakshas," she told the princes.

"A king?" said Lakshman, exchanging glances with Ram.

"Yes," replied Shurpanak. "Ravan the most powerful, having received a boon from Lord Brahma himself, giving complete protection from gods and demons."

Inside the cottage, Sita heard voices, and wandered outside carrying a basket of flowers. When she saw Shurpanak, she quickly moved closer to Ram.

"Who is this?" asked Shurpanak.

"This is my wife, Sita," replied Ram.

Shurpanak became agitated, her eyes ablaze with jealousy and loathing.

"When I first saw you," Shurpanak said, turning to Ram, "I was immediately attracted. It is not every day I meet such a strong, courageous, and good-looking specimen. I am sure you will satisfy all of my desires. This person you call a wife is nothing but a skinny bag of bones," she hissed. "I shall devour her, then we can wander the forest together."

Ram, highly amused at the developing situation, picked a flower from Sita's basket, leaned on his bow and crossed his leg, idly twirling the bloom between thumb and forefinger.

"Mistress, I must admit though you are an attractive one, but I regret to remind you, I am already married, so it would not be proper to take another wife, even if I desired one. So I am, unfortunately, unavailable. But do not be disappointed. Take my brother here," he added, looking at Lakshman.

Lakshman's smile faded instantly, but, grinning, Ram continued, aware that Lakshman was gazing at him aghast. "He's a good soul, a lot younger than me and just as strong, if not as handsome, a most agreeable personality. Trained in the arts, sciences, and etiquette, and more importantly, able, ready, and willing to take on a new wife, he will make you a fine companion."

Since Ram had rudely refused her, Shurpanak decided Lakshman would make an ideal second choice. She stared at him lustily and gurgled.

"O personification of beauty," stammered Lakshman, "do not be taken in by my brother's banter. He is a noble Prince and first in line to the throne of Ayodhya. I am only his humble servant, attending his many needs both day and night without respite or reward. Insist on Ram, he's your perfect match."

Shurpanak, although slow to pick up on the brother's light-hearted attitude, now realized they had been teasing her, and erupted angrily. "Arrggh, enough of this! You try my patience! I am sister of Ravan, and no one makes a fool out of me. I always get what I want, and no wispy-waisted slip of a girl is going to stand in my way!"

Her eyes bulging, she lunged at Sita, clawing at her throat with her nails, forcing Ram to take action. He immediately positioned himself between them.

"Lakshman!" Ram shouted, pushing her away. "This monster needs a lesson!"

Lakshman drew his knife, stepped forward, and in three deft movements severed Shurpanak's ears and nose from her head.

Shurpanak froze, feeling a strange numbness about her head, and looked down, staring in horror at the ground before her. There, staining the soft sand bright red, lay her flesh. She spun around, and wailing in agony, tore off into the forest.

CHAPTER 21

KHARA AND DUSHANA

DELIRIOUS WITH PAIN, STUMBLING, running, screaming and crying, Shurpanak sped on through the forest, hardly aware of where she was going, trying to stem the flow of blood from her wounds with strips of cloth torn from her clothing.

"Those two will pay!" she screeched. "Pay with their lives they will!"

Shurpanak ran many miles back along the trail beside the lake, looking for her brothers. "Khara! Dushana!" she screamed. "Where are you?"

Coming upon their camp, well hidden among the trees, Shurpanak stormed in, her clothes hanging off her, ripped to shreds by jungle thorns.

"Khara! Dushana! Help me!" she screamed, her wild red hair matted with blood.

A heavy-set warrior appeared. It was Khara.

"Is that you, sister?" he demanded. "Who has done this to you?"

"It was the sons of Dasarath," she croaked. "They attacked me!"

""By the gods! Dushana!" Khara called out, and a huge warrior, with arms like tree trunks, appeared. "Our sister has been mutilated by rebels. Get the physician at once, then bring the army to battle readiness! Where did this happen, sister?"

"At a cottage in the Panchavati," she cried as the physician, a short, fat warrior arrived to dress her wounds. Their names are Ram and Lakshman. They live like ascetics, but act like criminals! But beware, brother, they are expert warriors."

"We'll be careful," her brother assured her.

"They must die for this outrage!" Shurpanak wailed. "If it wasn't for that skimp, Ram's wife, I'd be marrying into the Ishvakhu line!"

"Don't worry, sister," Khara said, "my fourteen thousand warriors will descend upon them. They won't stand a chance."

Khara watched proudly as his warriors assembled, armed with spears, axes, bows, clubs, knives and swords. His broad-shouldered fighters stood in formation, ready for battle, waiting for the order.

"Dushana, we shall flatten Panchavati and cut its inhabitants to pieces!" he announced. "This is the price for maiming our sister. Let the transgressors pay for it in full! Lead off, I'll follow in my chariot."

Khara, never defeated in battle before, was in confident mood, intent on revenge. He raised his hand, and at the flick of his wrist, the entire army started forward, snaking its way through the forest towards

Panchavati. As they approached, the sky turned black, and thunder rumbled overhead.

***

As Sita, Ram, and Lakshman walked in the woods some distance from the cottage, an arrow thudded into a tree next to them, followed by a hail of projectiles.

"We're being attacked!" Ram shouted, pushing Sita to the ground. "Lakshman, take Sita to that cave and return to give me cover."

The forest filled with the sound of trumpets, drums, the clash of cymbals and war cries, as hordes of yelling rakshas attacked from all sides. Infantrymen, elephant troops, and cavalry swarmed through the clearings, weapons in hands and victory in their hearts.

Unstoppable.

A trumpet sounded, followed by a hail of arrows, along with axes, tridents and spears. Ram calmly defended himself, brushing aside missiles as they rained down on him, facing the continual barrage undaunted.

Each time he pulled back his bowstring; a wondrous sound reverberated through the forest. Khara's men stopped to listen, and as they did, Ram and Lakshman fired their deadly arrows, felling many huge trees, crushing hundreds of them.

Ram saw Khara give orders to attack, and the army, spread out across the forest, moved forward.

Ram took pity on them, knowing they unlucky and had but short lives. Bending his bow almost double, he let fly a deadly assault of arrows, one arrow merged into the next. Rakshas fell in hordes. First five. Then ten. Then scores. Their dying cries drowned out by the constant whine of arrows from Ram's majestic bow. Row after row of demons fell like scythed corn, blood from their shredded bodies turning into rivers that flowed across the forest floor.

Shurpanak, her wounds now bandaged, ran through the forest towards the sound of battle, hoping to witness the end of Ram and Lakshman. When she saw flashes of light pulsating through the trees, punctuated by horrific screams, she stopped and smiled.

Dushana returned Ram's fire, but Ram cut down his arrows as they sped towards him. Dushana moved closer, eager for a hit, but Ram had plans for him, sending a volley so powerful, that it tore Dushana's arms from his body, felling him like an ox.

In response, the rakshas army surged forward again, releasing more arrows at Ram and Lakshman. But despite all their efforts, they could not stop the brothers from dispatching half a dozen generals before finally finishing off most of the remaining soldiers.

Mad with a thwarted desire for revenge, Khara rushed forward with the last of his troops. Ram responded with arrows covered in gold and jewels, whose combined effect was even more devastating than before. Bodies, bits of armor and weapons flew through the air. Limbs and broken chariots littered the battlefield, as the remaining soldiers met their grisly end, twisted in agony, riddled by Ram's arrows, their lifeblood seeking its freedom on the hard earth, except for one lucky general, Akampan, who miraculously avoided Ram's arrows of death, and quickly made his escape.

At the end, Khara stood alone. He fired at Ram, and then prepared another arrow, but Ram's astra was already on its way. The projectile found its mark, Khara's vision clouded, and his bow slipped from his blood stained hands.

Then Ram sent another, this time, a donation from Indra. The blazing fire arrow struck the unfortunate Khara, and reduced him to ashes.

When Shurpanak entered the clearing, she saw the smoking corpses of her brother's army, and let out a piercing scream. There was no sign of Sita, Ram or Lakshman.

Gurgling in horror, she turned and ran back into the forest.

CHAPTER 22

RAVAN, KING OF THE RAKSHAS

WHEREVER THERE IS A positive, there is a negative. Whenever there is happiness, there is distress, and where there is good, there will always be evil.

The demoniac are usually engaged in horrible activities meant to destroy the world. Bereft of intelligence, they lord it over the material nature, in which they create havoc, their only interests being the accumulation of material possessions, and the pleasure of the flesh.

They have so much wealth, yet they go on scheming to acquire more, thus their plans for the world are never finished, and they continually engage in usurping and exploiting the masses.

They kill their enemies, or anyone who tries to stop them.

This hostility increases until it becomes uncontrollable, resulting in divisions first between individuals, families, societies, then eventually, nations, resulting in conflagration, and bloody war.

By performing sacrifices and worshipping *Devas*, they think they can gain personal benefit. By advertising themselves as God, they expect worship from others.

One such demon lived, who could not be vanquished.

His name was Ravan, King of Lanka.

Ravan himself was an awesome sight, tall, broad shouldered, and powerful. His body bore the scars of many battles, including one left by Indra's thunderbolt, one by Vishnu's discus, and another by Airavata the elephant, who had left his mark across the demon's chest. After spending ten thousand years in meditation and austerity, Ravan had pleased Lord Brahma, and therefore asked for immunity from death by any creature, except man, which he did not consider a threat.

Ravan delighted in inflicting cruelty on others and torturing his helpless victims. His name actually meant, "one who causes grief for others."

Ravan also had many wives, but none of them could satisfy him. His subjects, even his own brothers, feared him. Whatever he demanded, it was done. The heavenly Nandan garden and the Chaitrarath forest had been destroyed by his hand, and the course of the sun and moon hindered by his wrath.

Now Ravan sat on his throne, goblet in hand, scratching his thick, black beard, his dark eyes intent on the dancing women.

"Faster. Faster!" he growled. "That way! That way!"

The dancers went faster, the music reached a crescendo, and two of the dancers fell, bringing down the rest. Ravan scowled, and took a long drink from a silver goblet, full to the brim with red wine.

"You have failed to entertain me!" he thundered just as the throne room door flew open, revealing a disheveled, blood spattered Shurpanak. Two guards tried to bar her way.

"Out of my way, scum!" she yelled, throwing them aside as the music stopped.

Shurpanak made her way unsteadily towards Ravan, who stared at her through an alcoholic mist.

"Who are you?" he demanded.

"Are you so stupid that you don't recognize your own flesh and blood when it appears before you?" Shurpanak exclaimed. "What sort of a brother are you? Can you not see I am mortally wounded?"

"Shurpanak! What has happened to you?" Ravan cried, stepping down from his throne. "Who has done this?"

"The same two who killed your brothers, Khara and Dushana, and annihilated their entire army!"

"What! Khara and Dushana! My army wiped out! Who are these warriors?"

"Ram and Lakshman, the sons of Dasarath. Our sworn enemies!" Shurpanak screamed. "They roam the Dandaka forest at will, fearing no one, indiscriminately killing our people whenever they find them. They must be stopped. Send them to hell, Ravan."

The door opened, and General Akampan staggered in, followed by maidservants carrying medical dressings.

"My lord, there has been a great catastrophe," he gasped. "All our troops on patrol in the Dandaka. Finished! Fourteen thousand warriors! Khara and Dushana are no more."

Ravan's eyes grew red hot; his torso expanded in rage.

"I will twist them on skewers and hang them over a fire!" he exclaimed.

"It was just two men," said Akampan.

"Did they fight in alliance with Indra or other demigods?"

"No, they fought alone."

"The dynasty has been insulted!" spat Ravan, pacing up and down in a rage.

"This Ram possesses celestial weapons," Akampan told him, "and he can launch an arrow quicker than the eye can see."

"All fourteen thousand of my finest troops!" bellowed Ravan. "I pray you are not making this up, Akampan! Or you will surely join my illustrious soldiers!"

"I speak the truth, Your Majesty. This Ram must be a demigod, otherwise how would it have been possible for him to inflict so much destruction?"

Ravan picked up a goblet, and took a long drink before approaching Shurpanak, now recovering in the corner, her head wrapped in bandages.

"My dear sister," he said, "Tell me, what happened out there?"

"I was wandering through the forest when I came upon a cottage," she told him in a snarl. "It wasn't there last time I passed, so I hid and watched. Then I saw the prince named Ram. I've never seen such fine specimen, handsome as a god, with well-formed thighs and graceful legs, rippling muscles and lotus eyes. I desired him immediately, and approached the hut, intent on making him mine. But before I could cast my spell, his wife appeared. Oh, Ravan, she must be the most beautiful creature in all the universes," continued Shurpanak.

"How beautiful?"

"A goddess," retorted Shurpanak. "Shapely body, long black hair, lips as red as cherries. Her name is Sita. But, beware, brother, she will totally enchant you."

Ravan sat there, seeing Sita quite clearly in his mind. He could even begin to smell her.

"I lost control and went for her," Shurpanak told him. "But before I could reach her, Ram's brother, Lakshman, took his knife to me. Teach these mortals a lesson, brother. A lesson they'll never forget! Kill them both! Then take this Sita to your bed and make her your wife!"

From that moment on, Ravan knew what had to be done. He sat alone in his dark chambers many days and nights, planning revenge, and how to possess Sita.

CHAPTER 23

MARICHI THE WIZARD

IN THE EERIE AFTERGLOW of a Lanka sunset, the demon King made his way to the palace stables, home to a golden chariot drawn by goblin-headed mules.

Ravan boarded, and, at the crack of his whip, the chariot soared heavenwards, slicing through the evening mist, and disappeared into the gathering gloom, heading for the abode of the wizard, Marichi.

Ravan passed over some of the most wonderful lands and set down in a forest near a large tree. Nearby sat a hut covered in lichen and moss, which looked a thousand years old.

Marichi the wizard, dressed in a colorful gown, and wearing a long flowing beard, sat beside a bubbling cauldron in the apothecary, huddled over a mass of vials. He listened to a book machine, pushing down on each line in turn, sometimes pausing to converse with half a dozen tiny, squeaking rakshas demons living in the lab.

"This potion, my friends, will curl your toes. It's for friends, and it's for foes! He! He! He! He! He!" he said, picking up a beaker full of amber liquid.

Dipping his fingers into the beaker, he was about to sprinkle the potion over his shoulder, when the door imploded, and Ravan stormed in.

"Why didn't you knock?" Marichi demanded, jumping up in fright. "I nearly had a heart attack!"

"And waste my time? I have a job for you, you little weasel," Ravan thundered.

"You have, my lord?" Marichi said, groveling and rubbing his hands together. "Will you take refreshment first?"

"Marichi, I want your help," Ravan said, rudely ignoring the offer. "Someone calling himself Ram of Ayodhya is making trouble for me in the forest. He and his brother single-handedly sent my brother's Khara and Dushana, and their entire army of fourteen thousand brave warriors to Yamaraja, the Lord of Death! He also mutilated my sister Shurpanak, and threatens the lives of my fellow citizens, who cannot travel freely without fear of these rebels, who have the audacity to call themselves princes." He spoke grimly, determined to punish Ram. "He lives in our territory," he went on, "doing as he pleases, a so-called ascetic, while committing great acts of violence! My sister has been maimed for life by this monster. I want a trick from you, Marichi."

"I am forever at your disposal, my lord."

"Good! This Ram has a wife, a most beautiful creature. You will help me make her my own!"

Marichi's face turned gray with foreboding.

"My lord," he muttered, "that could be a mistake."

"I want a spell, not your opinion," snarled Ravan.

"O mighty Ravan, King of Lanka, your words fill me with dread," the wizard said. "I have heard of Ram, he is a great ksatriya, skilled in the art of warfare, and known all over the three worlds. It will be dangerous to engage with him. Even if you succeed, this plan will only bring death and destruction upon your dynasty."

"Your petty reasoning will get you hung, Marichi," retorted Ravan.

"Besides, my lord, there is no greater sin than to take another's wife. You cannot expect to fulfill this desire, which is, after all, born out of lust."

"You forget you're in the presence of the master, who can continue to give you life, or end it," snarled Ravan.

"Your Majesty," replied Marichi boldly, "there are forces bent on your destruction, otherwise why would they lead you to do these things. If you take Sita, you tread on the threshold of death itself. Ram will hunt you down, if it takes him all of eternity. There will be nowhere to run. You'll be cornered by a vengeful husband and slaughtered like a wild beast."

"Enough!" Ravan told him. "I didn't come here for your feeble lectures on morality, Marichi! Tomorrow you will accompany me to the forest. For this trifling favor, you will live. Refuse me and you die!"

"B-but Ravan, I have many duties to perform. Seven days must pass before I can oblige you."

Lunging at Marichi, Ravan grabbed him by the throat, lifting him off the ground with one hand.

"Listen old man," he growled. "Your life isn't worth a gutted rat's whisker. One word from me, and you cease to exist, so do not displease me. I want this done tomorrow. Do you understand?"

Ravan dropped Marichi, headed for the door and looked back.

"Tomorrow! Or you die!"

And then he was gone, slamming the door behind him, leaving Marichi squirming.

"Oh dear, what a predicament," he fretted. "If I go to the forest, Lord Ram will kill me. If I stay here, Ravan will kill me. Better to be killed by Ram."

The next day dawned beautiful and serene. Ravan woke early, ordered his chariot, and sped back to the house of Marichi.

"Come Marichi," he said. "Let us go to the Dandaka. And remember, do not fail me."

CHAPTER 24

THE ENCHANTED DEER

ONE CLOUDLESS, SUNNY MORNING, after they had finished their chores, Ram and Sita sat under a tree near their cottage, relaxing. Sita looked lovely in a yellow silk sari adorned with glittering ornaments, her hair studded with fresh lotus blossoms and jewels.

Since arriving in Panchavati, Sita had befriended some of the small forest animals. The larger animals were far too shy, and preferred to keep their distance, so Sita found it difficult to gain their confidence, but they did wander close by when no one was in sight, nibbling at small scraps of food left by Sita, as she watched, unseen, behind the cottage window.

But, it was the smaller animals Sita had the most affection for. When the little monkeys arrived, their babies clinging to them tightly, Sita was thrilled. She loved to watch the furry little bundles as they frolicked on the ground. Then there were the brightly colored birds, which she had trained to eat out of her hand. Sita loved to have them perch precariously on her shoulder, tickling her skin with their soft downy plumage, or blowing her hair across her face when they flew away.

"I made a new friend today," Sita told her husband, picking a handful of nuts. "Would you like to see him?"

And holding out a nut, she laughed as a squirrel jumped into her lap and grabbed it.

"You've made a friend for life, Sita," Ram told her as the creature scurried off.

"I saw it the other day, trying to steal our lunch off the table."

"It is so peaceful here, Sita," said Ram, looking around him.

As they sat there quietly, Sita turned, and saw, on the far side of the meadow, walking out of the trees, a deer that appeared to be glowing.

"Oh, Ram!" she cried, "A deer! And, look! It's shining!"

"Be still, Sita, or you'll frighten it," Ram told her, gazing at the animal. "Yes, it is indeed, an interesting sight."

The deer shone brightly, illuminating the ground around it as it munched on the grass. Its back freckled with thousands of sparkling jewels, glinting like a myriad of stars, sometimes golden, sometimes silver. Its underbelly was light blue, its sides, pale cream, and the tip of its tail was multi-colored, like a rainbow, and a garland of wild forest flowers hung round its neck. Even more wondrous was the fact that the deer continually changed color, shimmering like a phosphorescent aurora, now aquamarine, now golden.

Lakshman appeared beside Ram.

"What do you make of that, Lakshman?" he asked, as the deer changed color again.

"Rakshas magic," Lakshman said suspiciously. "Sita, I'd advise you not to go too near."

"Don't be silly, Lakshman," she said. "It's only a harmless deer. And it's hungry."

"It could be some kind of sorcery," Ram warned her.

"I've never seen anything like this before," stated Lakshman.

"I don't know what to make of it either," confessed Ram.

"Ram, can't you see, it's only a deer," said Sita impatiently. Will you catch it for me, please."

"Sita, we shouldn't meddle…"

"You know how much I love animals," Sita insisted, now with tears in her eyes. "I want it to be our mascot."

It hurt Ram so much to see Sita cry, and his heart filled with compassion.

"Ram, please!"

He exchanged glances with his brother and took a deep breath.

"Lakshman, stay here and guard Sita."

Ram ran towards the deer, which promptly jumped into a nearby thicket. Ram chased after it only to see it reappear nearby a few seconds later, and then vanish again.

The animal led Ram through leafy glades, and grassy meadows, past deep pools and across sparkling streams, continually disappearing and reappearing.

It played a clever game, and drew Ram, gradually, inexorably, away from the cottage. Very soon after, Ram lost his patience and decided to capture it. Waiting till it settled down, he rushed it, but the animal bounded away, head held high. When it reappeared once more, Ram placed an arrow in his bow, and fired, whereupon the deer went down, changing into the wizard Marichi, who with his dying breath, called out in Ram's voice.

"Sitaaaa! Lakshmaaan! Help me!" before vanishing into thin air. Then, one by one, the trees began to bend and sway in the direction of the cottage, carrying Marichi's voice along with them, like a woodland telegraph.

Ram quickly realized what was happening, and sprinted back through the forest as fast as he could go, determined to get to Sita before anything happened to her.

CHAPTER 25

THE WRATH OF SITA

OUTSIDE THE COTTAGE, SITA paced back and forth impatiently, waiting for Ram.

"Sita, the deer must have run further than we thought," said Lakshman, curiously watching the swaying trees.

"Why are those trees moving so strangely?" she asked.

"Sitaaaa! Lakshmaaan! Help me!"

"That's Ram's voice," cried Sita, putting a hand to her mouth. "He must be in trouble. Quickly, Lakshman, go and help him!"

"Ram can take care of himself, Sita," he said, resolutely.

"Lakshman, I implore you," said Sita, now agitated. "Help my husband!"

"Sita, Ram has ordered me to stay with you."

"Ram needs you, Lakshman," she pleaded with him. "He could be surrounded by hundreds of rakshas. They will kill him if you do not go!"

"That's not true, Sita. Ram can take care of himself, and has given me strict instructions. I cannot leave you under any circumstances."

Lakshman knew Ram didn't need his help. His brother was a power unto himself, a man who could destroy Khara, Dushana and their army without any trouble. But apparently, Sita did not share his confidence, and lost all her self-control.

"Ram is in grave danger," she shouted, "If he is harmed, you will be responsible!"

"Sita, my duty is to stay and protect you."

"What are you thinking about, Lakshman? Do you want Ram to die? Of course, that's it! You would rather let Ram die, so you can take his place!"

Lakshman had never seen Sita like this before.

"You stand there, acting like his friend," she cried, "but with Ram out of the way, you plan to make me your wife. Well, Lakshman, you will not succeed. I am totally devoted to my husband."

"Nothing could be further from my mind," said Lakshman, shivering. "My actions may seem strange to you, but…"

"I will always be true to Ram. No one can ever tear us apart! Go now, Lakshman, or, I'll kill myself!"

"Please do not talk like this," he begged her, "Ram has ordered me. I cannot leave you unprotected."

"I will take my life this very instant if you do not go and help my husband!" she yelled.

"Sita," Lakshman said, "are you not aware of the power of Ram? He is protected from birth. You saw yourself how he defeated single-handedly, Khara, Dushana, and their entire army. Ram has been lured away by a demon in disguise. I guessed that when I saw the deer. Somewhere out there, something is afoot. That's why I must stay with you. Ram will return soon. Then you'll see the truth in my statements."

"Lakshman, you are cold and unfeeling," she accused him. "You've planned this ever since Ram was banished to the forest. You even had a hand in it, his being banished, didn't you?"

Lakshman's jaw dropped and his arms went limp. He backed off, shifting on his feet.

"Your velvety words don't fool me," Sita continued, wringing her hands and leaning into Lakshman with a vengeance. "You're a rogue and a pretender. None of your wishes will come true. I would rather take my own life that let you touch me."

Sita's words shocked and pained Lakshman, even though he knew she was under the spell of *maya*.

"Mother Sita," he said, "You have always shown me great kindness. I have always had the highest respect for you, but your hurtful words enter my heart like fiery daggers…"

"You had better go, Lakshman. If you do not, I will jump onto a blazing fire, take deadly poison, or both! Then you will never get me."

Lakshman turned and cried. "Please Lord, help me. I cannot endure this torment a moment longer. I don't know what to do. The only path open for me is to leave Sita alone, and pray she comes to no harm."

Lakshman chanted a silent prayer. Then, bracing himself, he picked up his bow and prepared to leave.

"Stay within the confines of the cottage and you will be safe," he said, as he ran off into the forest.

But even as he left her, convinced he was doing the right thing, he was not certain his decision would hold well with Ram.

CHAPTER 26

THE DECEITFUL MENDICANT

As LAKSHMAN SPRINTED AWAY, Ravan appeared from behind a tree where he had been patiently waiting, a vantage point from which he had heard and seen everything, including the golden deer, which had so entranced Sita.

"Yes, Marichi will be well compensated by this display of delightful bewitchment," he thought, as he watched the dancing deer. "How easily Sita is pleased, just like a child. When we get to Lanka, her hardships will be over. She will have soft beds to sleep in, servants, and tasty rakshas food, freshly killed, especially for her. She can swim in the lakes and walk in the gardens. Yes, life for her was definitely going to get better. Marichi is certainly a performer. Yes, go on, tantalize her, make her want you."

Ravan remembered how exciting it was when Sita asked Ram to catch the deer for her, and of course he had complied, bounding after it, to be led further and further away.

Ravan had then observed Lakshman reacting to Marichi's voice, carried by the trees. When Ravan had heard Marichi's cry, he knew that he had met his end, which was as it should be. The wizard had lived and died to serve Ravan's purpose, and was therefore dispensable.

Ravan saw how Sita had become highly agitated, waving her arms at Lakshman, imploring him to go after Ram. He was so excited he found great difficulty keeping still. Soon, he would be celebrating.

When Lakshman ran off into the forest, Ravan was ecstatic.

After composing himself, Ravan stepped out of the bushes, cleverly disguised as a mendicant, wearing long red robes and chanting a Sanskrit prayer, a shiny staff from which hung a water pot, resting on his shoulder.

"This is going to be easy," he thought, as he approached the cottage. "Like picking flowers in a meadow."

At twenty-five yards, he could see inside the cottage, where Sita sat dabbing the tears from her eyes.

Another ten yards, and he could see the scanty furnishings against the back wall, and objects on the table. But then, when he was almost at the door, he encountered a force field so strong that it knocked him backwards.

"So Lakshman had left something behind for Sita's protection. What arrogance!"

And then Sita came to stand in the doorway, and Ravan stared in awe at her beauty.

Sita froze. The demon bowed.

"Blessing upon you, dear lady," he said.

The birds in the trees stopped chirping, the crickets stopped clicking, and a deep, engulfing silence descended upon the forest, as if every living thing had stopped to watch the drama unfold.

Not expecting to meet a holy man, Sita decided to welcome him, stranger though he was. According to tradition, sadhus were to be revered, and should be offered refreshments and a place to sit. In return you received their blessings. No one sent a sadhu away without first satisfying him.

"I've been walking in the forest all day," Ravan said, feasting his red eyes on her lovely form, "and am quite fatigued. Pray child, can you attend to my needs?"

For a moment Sita hesitated, then turned and walked gracefully into the cottage, giving Ravan's hungry eyes a chance to fill with the vision of her swaying hips beneath her swishing sari. Lust growing deep inside him, he spread his cloak on the ground, and sat down to chant his prayers.

Sita reappeared with a tray of refreshments, then paused on the threshold. Ravan could see the doubt creeping into her mind, but he continued to chant, and with each syllable of his prayers, she became more and more disarmed, and moved forward, stopping short of the monster.

"It is customary for the hostess to serve the guest," Ravan reminded her.

Sita placed the tray of food and drink on the ground.

"May the gods bless you and your family," said Ravan softly.

Ravan put the cup to his mouth and drank, before asking for her name.

"Sita!" he exclaimed, "what a delightful name. And what, may I ask, is someone as lovely as you doing here, living alone in the forest?"

"I am not alone, I live with my husband," she told him, glancing anxiously at the trees.

"I do not understand why you try to eke out an existence in this lonely, inhospitable place," he said, staring at her. "Forgive me, but I have never seen anyone so beautiful. You must have been sculptured by the gods themselves! Ha! Ha! Any man who leaves you alone in the forest doesn't deserve such a wife."

"My husband is faithful," she said uneasily, "and I love him. We are very happy."

"My lady, I doubt if you've experienced real happiness," he replied. "That's something you won't find in the forest."

"Ram is my only source of happiness," she said simply.

"Fair maiden, may I say that you are a most rapturous beauty, one who moves like a graceful swan."

Sita looked away, and the demon knew it was time.

"Have you heard of Ravan?" he said, and then, having drained his cup, threw it to the ground. "Renowned upholder of dharma," he snapped. "Master of mystical Arts, King of the Rakshas! I am the true source of real happiness!"

He rose and, as Sita watched, wide-eyed, slowly morphed before her eyes, transforming himself from a holy man into the demon King, complete with armor and weaponry. "And I have come to claim my prize," he declared.

"You are the sworn enemy of Kosala!" Sita cried, taking a step back.

"My dear lady, how can you say such a thing? I have Royal blood in my veins."

"I'll call my husband!"

"Ha! Ha! Ha! You can call all you want. I doubt you'll be heard."

Ravan then positioned himself between Sita and the cottage, and slowly started forward, forcing her to back up.

"I am the wife of Ram, the greatest warrior," she told him. "And, if you as much as touch me, my husband will deal with you most severely."

"Tut, tut, I have many wives, but none like you," Ravan replied, laughing heartedly. "You have spirit; I like that. In Lanka, you will be my queen, and all of your desires will be fulfilled. Gold, jewels, rare oils, beautiful clothes, and maidservants to take care of your every need. You will lack for nothing.

"You have nothing I want, Ravan!" she cried. "Ram is righteous, honorable and just. Upholder of the truth! Like a banyan tree, he gives shelter to those in need. Ram is a majestic lion, whose roar sends terror into the hearts of the jackals. You are less than a jackal, Ravan. Go back where you belong!"

Ravan's mirth gave way to violent erupting anger as he lunged at her, eyes glowing like red-hot coals. Struggling and kicking, Sita screamed in terror as Ravan grabbed her long hair, clamping a muscular arm around her waist. Jackals howled, and a huge bank of black clouds gathered in the sky.

"Ram, help me! Ram! Ram!" she screamed, flailing wildly at his face as he picked her up. "Let go of me, you monster!"

CHAPTER 27

THE ABDUCTION

RAVAN'S CHARIOT SUDDENLY APPEARED in front of the cottage, hovering an inch above the ground as he lifted Sita up with one hand, and swung her on board, kicking and screaming.

As the chariot shot upward, veering this way and that, Sita pummeled him in an attempt to loosen his vise-like grip, but Ravan simply laughed.

"Lakshman, O blameless one! Please help me," Sita cried over and over again until her strength gave out, and she slumped to the floor of the chariot, exhausted.

Ravan was elated.

"Ha, ha, my lovely," he chortled, "I see you have given up, a wise choice. I have much more to offer. For you, life is only just beginning."

Black clouds piled up and the sky darkened as they raced over the treetops, leaving Panchavati far behind.

Ravan was in a good mood. He had taken Sita without opposition. As he thanked the worshipful demigods for his success, he did not, at first, notice the small speck in the sky approaching until it was almost upon him.

Squawking madly, Jatayu launched himself straight at Ravan. Attacking with his sharp claws, he caused the chariot to swerve violently, nearly throwing Sita overboard.

"If it's a fight you want, you'll get it!" Ravan shouted, recovering quickly, as he drew his bow and fired. But Jatayu was too quick, and dodging the arrow, attacked again, this time breaking Ravan's bow and denting his armor. As the chariot bucked and weaved, Ravan groped for his sword, but Jatayu came round again, this time targeting the shining car itself, striking it with such force that Ravan lost all control. The chariot plunged down through the trees, landing with an almighty bump, and skidded to a halt on the grass, throwing Sita out. Hastily picking herself up, Sita made a dash for freedom, a furious Ravan close behind her.

Meanwhile, not far away, Ram, aware now that he had been deceived, hurried back towards the cottage along the narrow trail and met Lakshman coming towards him.

"Lakshman! He cried. "What are you doing here?"

"Are you alright?" his brother replied, "We heard your call for help."

"That was Marichi's voice. A clever trick to get me away from the cottage. Why did you leave Sita there alone?"

"Ram, I've always followed your instructions, but Sita said she would kill herself if I did not go to find you."

"Lakshman, I gave you clear instructions. You should not have left Sita."

"Oh, Ram. Sita was saying so many hurtful things. I had to leave."

"You should not have let her unkind words affect your judgment. Women say many things when they're angry."

"Brother, her cruel words cut right through my heart. I had no choice. I'm sorry Ram, but it was unbearable."

"Lakshman, your primary function is to protect. This is the duty of a ksatriya. You should not have deserted her, no matter what the provocation. Sita is wise. Had you waited until she composed herself, she would not have unleashed reckless words upon you. But we have wasted enough time. We must get back to the cottage right away.

***

Through the trees a few hundred yards away, Ravan closed fast on Sita, and ran her down. As he clasped her in his mighty arms, she uttered a scream that would stop Ram and Lakshman in their tracks.

High above the forest, Jatayu circled searching for Ravan. Seeing his chariot clear the trees once more, Jatayu closed rapidly. Judging the right moment to strike, he attacked, gouging the demon's arm with his talons, as he swept past.

"Arrgghh! By the gods!" Ravan bellowed in pain.

When Jatayu soared around again, Ravan tried to out-maneuver him by rocking and swaying, then, as Jatayu swooped down once more, he drew his huge sword and hacked. As cold steel cut to bone, Jatayu screamed, and fell onto the chariot, terribly injured, but still valiant enough to try peck Ravan, even as his life-blood spilled down the sides of the car. Stupefied, Sita could do nothing but watch in horror as Ravan raised his sword and brought it down, severing Jatayu's wing before booting him unceremoniously over the side. Spinning like a top, the brave bird plummeted to the ground far below.

"That'll teach you to tangle with me," Ravan said.

Sita watched as Jatayu fell, and then she threw herself on the floor, where she lay crying, and calling out to Jatayu.

"Oh Jatayu, brave Jatayu, you gave your life for me," she gasped.

After nursing his painful wounds, Ravan slapped the reins, pushing the chariot over the treetops, higher and higher, faster and faster, hurtling over interminable forest.

Lying on the floor, Sita spied a hole in the side of the car. Through it, she could see smoke rising from a hut far below. Checking to see Ravan wasn't looking, she wrapped her jewels in her scarf and flung them over the side, before sliding down into a corner for the rest of the journey.

By the time the forest gradually receded, giving way to barren plains and wasteland, and eventually, vast gray mountains, the exhausted Sita slept.

The coastline passed beneath them, and they flew out across a vast, dark ocean, on which white-capped waves formed long lines in the failing light. Thick, black clouds piled up overhead, lightning flashed on the horizon, and it started to rain.

Ravan cracked the whip now, driving the goblin headed mules relentlessly, while the chariot tossed in the heavy turbulence. Finally, through a gap in the clouds, Ravan saw a small island, and smiling, steered the craft toward a spot where strange foreboding cliffs rose up half a mile out of the sea.

As the chariot neared land, Ravan headed straight for a large promontory, shaped like a demon's head, entering a large cave hidden within the open mouth, eventually emerging over the magnificent city of Lanka, scraping and sliding across the roof of a golden palace. Ravan lifted the waking Sita out, where half a dozen ogress guards immediately surrounded her. He pushed her towards a guard with cat-like eyes.

"Trijata!" he called out. "Give her whatever she desires, clothes, perfume, jewels. Anything; except her freedom. Take very good care of this one, if you value your life."

"Yes, master," said the demoness, as she led the weeping Sita away.

As for Ravan, he headed straight for the Palace where he grabbed a passing general.

"Take eight warriors and go to Khara's last camp," he commanded him. Send out spies. I want the precise whereabouts of this Ram, and his brother, Lakshman! Their fate now rests in my hands!"

CHAPTER 28

SEARCH THE HIDING PLACES

RAM AND LAKSHMAN SOON reached the spot where they thought they heard Sita scream, and began an immediate search.

"There's no one here," Ram said finally. "We should return to the cottage."

"Could we have really come this far?" said Lakshman, looking around.

Ram hurried along, hardly aware of his brother's presence, with thoughts only for Sita's safety. If anything happened to her...

"I must get to Sita," Ram told himself. "What if a rakshas came and killed her."

Tears streamed down his cheeks as he raced back, trying desperately not to think of what he might find in the coming few minutes, hoping his beloved Sita was safe and well, peacefully going about her daily chores, waiting patiently for his return.

When they reached the clearing, they were met with a strange sight. All the vegetation, bushes, trees and flowers in the immediate vicinity had withered away. Where there once was greenery and color was now only devastation. Bolting inside the cottage, Ram found it deserted, except for a squirrel eating the rind of a coconut.

"Sita! Sita! Sita!" he shouted, rubbing his left eye, his voice echoing through the empty hut. "Sita, where are you?"

He saw she had been preparing a light meal, noting the fruit peelings still on the table.

"Sita is not here," he said, then went outside and saw Lakshman pointing at the trees.

"Look, Ram," said Lakshman, walking away. "Every single leaf has disappeared."

Ram looked towards the trees, just like when he had searched for Shurpanak, but this time, all the trees were devoid of foliage, leaving only gnarled, dry branches. Then he looked down and saw the upturned tray of food and drink.

"Someone has been here," he said.

"And here is Sita's hairpin." Lakshman shouted, picking an object off the ground.

"She must still be somewhere around," Ram whispered to himself. "She must be at the river, fetching water, or picking flowers in the forest."

Ram ran across the clearing to the riverbank calling Sita's name.

Silence. Nothing moved.

The brothers went down to the river and searched the area around the deep pool where they swam every day, and the glade where Sita picked flowers, but she was not there.

Desperate, Ram dropped to his knees and prayed to Lord Vishnu for Sita's safekeeping. Then he started a systematic search, looking in all the special hideaways, the little places where they would sit and talk together telling each other stories, or lie gazing at the sky and listening to the forest. But each time he was met with disappointment.

"Perhaps Sita has gone a little further in search of berries or roots," he said to Lakshman. "You look in that direction, and I'll go over there. We'll meet back at the cottage."

Lakshman blamed himself. If only he had been more obstinate and stayed with Sita, this would never have happened, and he desperately tried to make it up to him by conducting a thorough search in the surrounding forest.

The brothers looked in every place they knew in the vicinity of the cottage, but still they could not find her.

"We must accept the fact that Sita has gone," Lakshman said, when they met again, whereupon, Ram, overcome with grief, called her name over and over again.

"Is it not enough to lose the throne and be banished to the forest for fourteen years?" wailed Ram, "Now I am parted from my dearest wife, who might be meeting her end at this very moment."

"No, brother," argued Lakshman, trying desperately to console him, "there are many more hiding places in this forest left for us to search. Sita may have taken to any one of those. Do not give up so easily. Sita is around somewhere."

"I have to believe she has been abducted," Ram said soberly.

Knowing that he could not alleviate his brother's distress, Lakshman vowed, there and then, not to rest until Sita had been found.

As the brothers rested outside the cottage in the late afternoon sun, a small group of deer appeared, and wandered close by. In desperation, Ram called out to them.

"Tell me your secrets, simple creatures. Did you see what happened? Do you know where Sita is? Where did she go? Please tell me."

A number of small deer came close to Ram.

"If only you could talk," he groaned.

The animals could not understand the torment of the divine Ram, but knew he was appealing to them for help. The deer milled around in front of the cottage, ears twitching, tails swishing, and Ram saw to his amazement that first one and then another and another turned their heads in one direction. Having a great love and respect for all animals, Ram understood this odd behavior.

"Look, Lakshman!" he said excitedly, "they're pointing to the south. That's where Sita is! They must have seen something and are trying to tell us. Come on let's search in that direction. It's our only chance."

Ram and Lakshman ran off into the forest and began to search. A few moments later, Lakshman discovered a pile of flowers scattered across the path. Ram's hand was shaking as he picked one up.

"Lakshman, the deer were right," he said. "These are the lotus blossoms Sita put in her hair this very day!"

The brothers searched around for Sita's footprints, but found nothing. They spread out and scoured every inch of the immediate area, hoping to find some other signs that she had been there until finally, as Lakshman searched the brush to the right, they came upon pieces of twisted metal, shining like burnished brass, lying scattered on the ground. A broken bow, and a quiver full of broken arrows, along with the shattered remains of bloody armor, covered in long scratches, lay close by.

Had this been the end of Sita? Had she been killed here, and then dragged somewhere else? Ram found it difficult to speak. And then he came upon a huge sword with a broken blade, its hilt covered in jewels and precious stones.

"This is a rakshas sword," he told his brother, nearly choking on the words. "There have been demons here. Oh Sita!"

They moved further south, and as they hacked their way through dense undergrowth, they heard a long sigh.

Drawing their swords, the brothers started cutting their way into the thicket. Then Ram saw the bird lying in the bushes, covered in blood, barely alive.

"It's Jatayu!" Lakshman cried. "He's been hurt!"

Ram knelt beside Jatayu, and stroked his bloodied neck.

"Jatayu," he said, as the giant bird raised his head and implored help with his eyes. "What happened to you?"

"Oh, Ram," his voice rose just above a whisper. "Sita has…"

"Did you see Sita?"

"I tried… to save the… Princess Sita. But she has gone. Forgive me. The demon… Ravan. He took her."

Ram turned to his brother. "Lakshman, do you hear that! Ravan has her! I have to find out where he's taken her!"

"Careful Ram," Lakshman advised, "Jatayu has lost a lot of blood."

But Ram knew that their dying friend had more to say.

"What did you see?" he asked him. "Where did Ravan go? Please try to tell me, Jatayu, I beg you."

But it was too late. Jatayu gave up his life there and then, his battered body unable to endure the terrible injuries, and his soul departed like a wisp of smoke, its karma taking it to a higher ground, a fitting end for such a devoted creature.

Ram, remembering the first time he met Jatayu in the alien forest, and the promise the vulture had made to protect Sita, buried his head in his hands, and wept until, gathering resolve, he began to collect wood to cremate him. As the pyre blazed, Ram prayed, paying homage to his brave friend, Jatayu, protector of Sita.

"I shall never forget you, brave Jatayu," he said when it was time to go. "Not as long as I live."

The brothers went back to the cottage, to pick up supplies, and then started out on their search for Sita.

***

Day after day they tramped through the forest, looking for Sita.

"How long have we been searching?" asked Ram one morning.

"I'm not sure, maybe just over a week," replied Lakshman, looking compassionately at his brother who was clearly suffering.

From then on, they started each new day in the same way; rising early to bathe in a nearby pool or stream, followed by a period of meditation and prayers, then breakfast. After this, plans were made for the day's search. They discussed their progress, and planned where they would go and what they could do to quicken the rate of search towards the south.

Gradually, their travels took them to higher ground, and they left the misty forest landscape below them, Ram calling Sita's name constantly as they slowly made their way up the long trails, his voice echoing poignantly, far out across the miles.

As they journeyed on, they met various sages, and stayed at various hermitages along the way, taking shelter and nourishment from the ascetics. Each time they stopped at an ashram, Ram told them his sad story.

The weeks turned into months, but still they did not find any sign of Sita. The sun changed its course, setting lower in the sky, and a cool breeze blew through the forest, scattering dead leaves underfoot. The nights became colder, forcing the brothers to beg thicker clothing from those sages they met. And although neither of them complained, the pain of their loss was there to see in their eyes.

The brothers began to enter a remote part of the Dandaka Forest. Stretching for over a thousand miles in every direction, it was a land large enough to swallow entire civilizations, and as they searched, it grew darker and denser. It was then that they heard the calls of strange creatures. On one occasion, Lakshman saw an elephant with large tusks. They could tell it was alien country by the many strange things they saw.

Ram began to despair that he would never see Sita again, and the frustration of not finding her burned him up.

"Ram, do not let your failure to find Sita affect you," consoled Lakshman. "She is no ordinary mortal. Remember that she is always under the protection of Vishnu."

But nothing could dampen Ram's spirit or break his resolve in his quest to find Sita. His determination increased with each day.

He could not live without her.

CHAPTER 29

HANUMAN

ABOUT MID MORNING ON the following day when the brothers were well on the trail again, they found themselves in a damp, ancient riverbed, sunk between ivy-covered trees. It was quiet, and the ground was covered with a fine layer of brown conifer needles. The tang of resin mingled with the smell of musty leaves and damp moss pervaded the entire area, the absence of bird song adding to the eerie atmosphere. In the half-light, nothing moved.

Lakshman heard a rustling sound, and stopped to listen. When the crack of a breaking branch reached them, they proceeded cautiously, but, when they heard a heavy thud, both princes stopped dead in their tracks and drew their swords. Up ahead, the path curved round the thick trunk of a tree, where, rounding it, they came face to face with a six-foot monkey, armed with a mace.

"What on earth!" Lakshman exclaimed, stopping dead, while Ram instinctively dropped his sword, and took up his bow, sliding an arrow into place.

"Let us pass," he declared.

"My dear sirs," said the monkey, standing his ground, "I wouldn't dream of impeding your desire to roam freely in the forest, even in the slightest. But let me warn you. There are dangers here you should be aware of. Ignorance has spelt disaster for many a traveler."

"We are not afraid of anything," Lakshman told him, quickly recovering, "nor are we in ignorance. We are on a mission."

"What my brother means is, we are trying to find my wife," Ram explained, eyeing the stranger with interest. "She has been abducted by a demon."

"I am sorry to hear that," said the monkey. "What is your name?"

"I am Ramachandra, and this is my brother, Lakshman. We are the sons of King Dasarath of Ayodhya."

"I'm Hanuman, son of the Wind God, Vayu, and Commander-in-Chief in the monkey army.

"Monkey army?" repeated Lakshman.

"I am honored Hanuman," said Ram. "We have been searching for many months now, and still we have no clue as to my wife's whereabouts. Since she disappeared from our cottage in Panchavati, we have searched this interminable forest, without success."

"Why don't you come with me?" Hanuman said, a large grin spreading across his anthropoid face. "I'll take you to our king, Sugriva. He lives on Rishyamukhya Hill. I'm sure he would be pleased to help you."

"Can we trust him, Ram?" Lakshman said in a low voice.

"Yes, Lakshman. He seems like a decent kind of fellow."

As Hanuman loped off, closely followed by the two brothers, Lakshman took a deep breath, bolstered by a new hope that Sugriva might help him find Sita.

CHAPTER 30

KISHKINDA, CITY OF THE MONKEYS

FOR THE REST OF the day they trekked through the jungle, avoiding wild creatures and ferocious animals until, towards late afternoon, Hanuman gestured for them to follow him up a narrow forest path. When they reached the top, Hanuman pointed to the sky. Looking up, they saw, high up on the side of a cliff, hidden amongst the trees, a magnificent wooden city.

"Fantastic!" Lakshman exclaimed, as he saw palaces and walkways, blending into the giant banyan trees.

Hanuman waited for them to take it all in, before uncovering a hidden rope ladder which spiraled skyward, precariously clinging to the ancient trees.

"Welcome to Kishkindha," Hanuman called back to them, as he started to climb, swinging easily up the ladder.

It was a tough climb up, but exciting. The higher they went, the more they saw. Soon they were out of breath, panting at the effort to attain the first level, where they found it was guarded by large monkeys. Higher up, other levels could be seen, stretching on forever. On the second level, they reached the main city gate, guarded by armored, bulky monkey warriors, who challenged them before letting them step through the fortified doorway. They followed Hanuman across a long rope bridge connecting the two halves of the city, and entered a courtyard leading to a giant palace.

Monkey guards and citizens watched them arrive, looking at the two humans with interest, many never having seen Homo erectus before. Ram and Lakshman were welcomed by the head of the guards and then by monkey ministers, before being escorted by Hanuman into the palace.

"Wait here," said Hanuman, as he entered the throne room.

The palace itself was marvelously engineered, with architecturally superior teak carvings, walls and floors throughout. And when they followed their new friend into the throne room, they saw a powerfully built, gray monkey, dressed in yellow robes and a gold battledress encrusted with precious stones, waiting for them. He sat on an impressive wooden throne with a golden crown on his head.

"Your Majesty," said Hanuman, "I have brought two warrior sons of King Dasarath, to see you. Sita, the wife of Ram, was taken from their cottage in the forest, possibly kidnapped by a rakshas demon. The prince and his brother come to ask for your help."

"Welcome to my city," said Sugriva, smiling. "You will find it strange at first, but do not worry. You will become accustomed to it. I have heard of you, Prince Ram, and your great deeds."

"I am pleased to meet you, Majesty," said Ram, bowing.

"All the mystics know of Ram," continued Sugriva, "he's the enlightened one. Now how can I help you?"

"Your Majesty," said Ram, "in Panchavati a few months ago, my wife was forcibly abducted by the demon, Ravan."

"Yes, we have heard of this Ravan, a barbaric evil-doer. You mentioned Panchavati?"

"Yes. That's where our cottage is."

"One of our scouting parties found a little bundle in that area a while ago," said Sugriva, and motioned to one of his aides. "Bring it here."

Ram took the bundle and untied it with shaking hands. When he saw what was inside, he fell to his knees.

"It's Sita's hair pin and jewelry," he cried. "Oh Sita."

Jambavan, the old black bear, and minister to Sugriva, offered his support. "Don't worry Prince Ram," he said gruffly, giving him a reassuring pat on the shoulder, "Sita will be found."

"You see," Sugriva informed the grieving prince. "We know where Ravan has his city, a fortress across the sea on the island of Lanka. Yes, young Angada. What is it you want?"

Sugriva's nephew, Prince Angada, planted himself squarely in front of the throne. "We should all go to Lanka, kill these rakshas and rescue Sita!"

"Now let's take one thing at a time Angada, my son," said Jambavan, "I know you can't wait to have a go, but we need to get an order first."

"But, there is one important thing," Sugriva continued, "We may not find Sita in Lanka. Ravan has many rakshas acquaintances scattered across this earth, and she may be with one of them. But wherever she is, she will be under heavy guard."

Ram was becoming more depressed by the minute. "King Sugriva," he said, "you must excuse us. We have to be on our way."

"You will find the going difficult," the monkey king informed Ram, as he turned to leave. "In a few days the rains will come and flood the forest, making travel almost impossible. We are prepared for the monsoon. You would be wise to stay here until the rains stop. When they do, we will help you find your Sita."

"I am most grateful, Your Majesty."

Later that night, a mighty flash of lightning exploded across the mountain, immediately followed by a clap of thunder, heralding the arrival of the monsoon. The heavens opened, and released torrents of water that cascaded down through the trees, flooding the forest floor far below. A melancholy Ram sat by a window, looking out onto the sodden, dripping landscape.

While the brothers waited for the rains to end, Sugriva put everything at their disposal, showing great compassion towards the grieving Prince.

For many weeks, gray walls of water swept down the slopes of the mountains, drenching the parched land, filling the dry washes, before swelling into the rivers that surged down to the coast, many miles away.

Day after day, Ram looked through his window at the rain, its roar filling his eardrums, its longevity, dashing his hopes, and his thoughts raced back to the times they had together at the cottage. How happy they had been then, roaming the forest all day, picking wild fruits and flowers, watching the flamingos, or cooling off in the deep pool down by the river.

"Oh Sita," Ram mused to himself, "you had put up with the hardships of the forest for many years, a hut for a home instead of a palace. But what are you suffering now, taken from me by an evil force? How I wish I could restart time itself."

***

The monkeys warriors were dispersed all over the land, and had to be recalled before a search could be mounted. Sugriva held a meeting to organize envoys to bring them back.

"You will inform each and every trooper to immediately return to Kishkinda. You will go to the mountains of Himavan and Kailasa, and the hills of Mahendra and Mandara, to the seashores and forests both near and far. You will visit those who live in the cities, the caves, the woods, the coasts, valleys, lakes and plains. Tell them they must return immediately, ready to march as soon as the weather breaks. Soon, there will be an army the like of which has never been seen before."

From a window in the palace, Ram watched the envoys depart in the pouring rain, trudging off into the wet, gray gloom, which mirrored the despair that filled his heart.

When eventually, the rains stopped, the sun broke through the black, water-laden clouds, shining on every tiny droplet of rain that hung from every branch, leaf and flower, turning them into dancing, sparkling lights.

Steam slowly rose from the wet forest floor, producing a thick mist, as sunlight filtered through the dripping trees, displaying thousands of shimmering, dancing colors. Birds sang, monkeys chattered loudly, and the whole animal world began to fill the forest with sound.

A week later, the first of the monkey warriors began to arrive in Kishkinda. From the mountain ranges, hillside dwellings and hermitages they came, numbers swelling by the hour.

Ram and Lakshman went onto the palace roof to join Sugriva and Hanuman, to witness the arrival of hundreds of thousands of wet, muddy, monkey warriors who had made the long, hard journey from the four corners of the land. Ram was overcome with emotion, and waved to them, shouting, "Victory to the Monkey Army!"

Immediately, every spear and sword was raised in response, and Ram, admiring the spectacle of monkey warriors spread out as far as the eye could see, solemnly made a promise that each and every one of them would receive his complete protection. In the throne room, monkey generals, officers and ministers assembled for briefing, joined by Ram, Lakshman and Hanuman, as Sugriva began to organize the search parties.

"I am sending twenty thousand warriors," said Sugriva, "split into four divisions, who will each search in a different direction. General Satabali, you will proceed north, General Sushena, I want you to go west, Vinata, you will go east, and Hanuman, you will go south. You will search all the lakes, mountainsides, forests, caves, watering places, streams, dales, groves, cities, islands, riverbanks, seashores and hill forts. When you find Sita, do not attempt a rescue, but return with her exact location. The entire Monkey Army will then march to her aid. Remember, you have exactly one month to bring us your news, good or otherwise."

After the assembly dispersed, Sugriva took Hanuman aside.

"Hanuman, as son of Vayu, you are possessor of supernatural strength and extraordinary powers. I believe Sita to be somewhere in the south. That was the direction she was going when she dropped the bundle. If you find her in Lanka, return with a report of Ravan's troop numbers and positions. Success or failure of our mission may depend on the information you bring us."

After Hanuman had left the throne room, Ram addressed him privately. "If you find Sita, please give her this signet ring," he said. "She will recognize it without difficulty. Tell her, I miss her very much. Tell her I am on my way, and that we'll soon be together again. You have speed and intelligence in your favor, Hanuman. Use them well, and may God protect you."

CHAPTER 31

IN SEARCH OF SITA

HANUMAN AND HIS DETACHMENT of monkey soldiers headed south, their search taking them through forests, over high mountains and across immense plains. They looked in caves, abandoned huts, ashrams, and mountain hideaways, until, after spending days hacking their way through dense jungle, they found themselves standing on a beach, where a glistening blue ocean, shimmering in the bright sunlight, obstructed them. The crash of waves on the golden sand seemed to entrance the monkeys, and they lay on the beach resting, while discussions took place between officers about what to do next.

"We cannot give up," Angada said, a stern look on his face. "We've come so far. Yet there remains only one week left before we must return and report to King Sugriva."

As the army waited, gazing at the pounding waves, an eagle appeared, high in the sky, circling above them before soaring down to land on the beach. Angad went to investigate, sword in hand.

"Who are you and what do you want?" he demanded.

"My name is Sampati, brother of Jatayu," the bird replied calmly.

"Jatayu? Why that's the creature who tried to stop Ravan!" exclaimed Angad, as Jambavan arrived.

"We have heard of your brother," said Jambavan sympathetically. "We are sorry, but Jatayu gave his life trying to save the Princess Sita."

"Oh, dear, that is sad," said Sampati.

"But, Jatayu fought bravely," continued Jambavan. "He tried to stop Ravan taking the Princess away. We are searching for her, but the ocean blocks our path."

"Jatayu's death must not be in vain," Sampati said, resignedly. "I think I can help. Some time ago, my son, Suparswa, saw a chariot flying in the direction of Lanka. It was carrying a beautiful young woman who might have been Sita."

"Tell us of this Lanka," asked Jambavan.

"I must warn you that the golden city of Lanka, built by Visvakarma, architect to the gods, is the fortress home of Ravan, and a very hostile place," Sampati replied in a slow, trembling voice, pointing across the sea as his jet black feathers ruffled in the breeze. "Lanka lies one hundred *yojanas* over there."

Jambavan called the monkeys together, and assembled them in front of him.

"We need to reach Ravan's island, a hundred yojanas away. Now, some of us can jump a good distance."

"But not over that ocean," said one monkey.

"There is only one person who can jump that distance, and that is you, Hanuman," Jambavan said. "Because, you're endowed with the mystic potency inherited from your father, Vayu, this jump to Lanka is well within your capabilities. If you leave now, you'll reach Lanka by nightfall. If you're not back by dawn, we will assume you have been captured."

"You're the only one who can do it," said Angad.

"Be careful, Hanuman. Lanka is heavily guarded," advised Jambavan.

"Well, what have I got to lose? If I don't fall into the ocean I'll probably be captured by Ravan's forces."

And, so it was agreed, that Hanuman would try to fly all the way to Lanka and search for Sita on his own, even though there would be many dangers, both on the way, and when he reached his destination.

Unperturbed, Hanuman, the junior servant of Hari, faced the sea, offered his obeisances and prayers unto the demigods, and meditated with folded palms. Then he took a deep breath, chanted a sacred mantra, and started to grow until he reached the height of many hundreds of feet. Some monkey warriors ran away in fear, but most, true believers, all stood their ground, and watched, awestruck, as seabirds soared around Hanuman as if he was some towering, rocky crag.

The monkeys stood well back as Hanuman bent his legs and sprung up from the ground, roaring with joy as he whipped up through the clouds like an arrow and disappeared over the horizon in the direction of Lanka.

CHAPTER 32

THE CITY OF LANKA

HANUMAN SKIMMED OVER THE ocean, flying at high speed, until he saw a strip of land in the distance. It was dusk when he passed over the coastline, where he saw a high range of mountains topped with two impressive peaks.

Eventually, the outline of a city appeared, protected by a colossal wall and surrounded by a wide moat, its buildings rising eight stories high, covered entirely with gold, the walls inlaid with jewels and precious stones. Hanuman realized, with growing excitement, that this must be the Golden City of Lanka.

He landed on a rock to get his bearings and to survey the scene, and saw streets full of people of different races, elephants, mules, ogresses, and thousands of armor-clad troops.

Knowing that Lanka was so closely guarded that not even the wind could enter the city without detection, he decided to find a safe landing place and wait until nightfall.

When it was dark, he took off again, approaching the outer wall of the city, but before he could reach it, he smashed into a force field.

As Hanuman picked himself up, a ghostly being with a shapely figure appeared out of the wall.

"You are unauthorized to proceed. State your name and purpose of visit."

"Who are you?" asked Hanuman, staring in disbelief.

"I am Lankini, guardian of the City of Lanka," said the apparition.

"I am Hanuman."

"What do you want?"

"I've heard so much about your great city, I've come to see it for myself."

"You do not fool me," replied Lankini. "You are a spy, and will be vaporized!"

Raising her arm, Lankini released a pattern of missiles towards Hanuman, who quickly leveled his mace and deflected them off into space, leaving pale blue trails across the night sky, after which he shattered the force field into a billion pieces with his mace, then flew off to land on a deserted balcony from which he could see the citizens of the city going about their business and scores of troops at every corner.

The more Hanuman saw, the more he was convinced that they would never fight their way in.

Having decided to get a more intimate view of the city, he folded his hands, chanted a prayer, shrunk to the size of a cat, and took off again to make a detailed inspection.

The evening was filled with the shouts of merchants and traders busy selling their wares. Drums and bugles sounded, and Hanuman heard melodious songs and laughter, and saw hundreds of beautiful women walking the streets, anklets tinkling and jewelry clinking. He heard the changing of the guard in the palace courtyard, the jangle of horse brass and armor on through the cobbled streets, and a beautiful woman singing from a window, accompanied by musical instruments.

He saw chariots, palanquins, and, in the sky, glowing aerial craft. Deer, horses, and four-tusked mammoths roamed the street, garlanded with jewels.

In the light of a waxing moon appearing low on the horizon, Hanuman took mental notes of the position of the gates; security huts, checkpoints, and the number of guards posted at each position as he passed overhead.

Flying lower to get a better view, he misjudged his approach and collided with a stall, landing in a vat of liquor. He struggled out and shook off the excess, coughing, spitting and gagging, disgusted by the vile tasting liquid.

He watched, amazed as the stallholder stepped out of the darkness, dipped a cup into the liquid, took a drink, and then offered it to a passing woman, who caressed the cup in her hands, giving him a long, alluring look, before drinking seductively.

Keeping an eye out for further obstacles, Hanuman flew off again, making a careful search of every street and square.

Hour after hour, street-by-street, house-by-house, he continued his search for Sita until he had covered the whole city, including every alleyway and dead end, after which he concluded that she must be somewhere in Ravan's palace itself. On arriving there, he found impenetrable sheer drops on either side, from which a fall would end in certain death. Still, he continued his search around the outside of the building, which began to shine eerily in the light of the rising moon.

Hanuman decided to begin his search on the top floors of the palace, and flying higher, he spotted a building topped with a golden roof. He flew through an open window, where guards were posted at each door. Apart from the sound of laughter, he heard nothing.

Outside, the moon rose, illuminating the palace in a ghostly pale light, reflecting on the cold streets and capstones, turning night nearly into day. Hanuman waited, before flying into a large, luxuriously fitted side room, the walls and ceilings adorned with gold and jewels, where men and women sprawled in drunken slumber. But none of the women matched Ram's description of Sita. Soon, he was convinced she was not there.

He went into another room, its walls encrusted with coral, gems and pearls, and incense filled the air. This time, he saw only beautiful women lying asleep on the floor, or on couches, seats and beds, all breathtakingly inlaid with gold, precious stones, ivory and sandalwood.

"This must be Ravan's harem," he whispered to himself.

Hanuman ventured further, gazing on their faces. He looked into each and every one, but none of them were Sita.

Upstairs, he noticed a coat of arms displayed on a door. Entering the room, he found a large white umbrella hanging from the wall over a huge white bed, constructed of ivory and crystal. Three figures reclined on it, two beautiful women, and a huge dark man dressed in white, with a long handlebar moustache, a man he knew at once must be Ravan. Hanuman looked at the women on the bed, and then concluded that Sita would not be found sleeping in the same building, let alone the same room as Ravan.

In another room, a mature woman of exquisite beauty, wearing exotic jewelry in her long black hair, lay on a single bed covered with golden cloth, a woman he thought must be a queen.

Hanuman looked around for the last time, and then left the palace. Once outside, he chanted a mantra and resumed his normal size as the last of the stars slowly faded in the growing light. As another day began there was still no sign of the woman on which Ram's happiness depended. Was he, Hanuman asked himself, fated to admit defeat?

CHAPTER 33

IN THE ASHOKA GROVE

"OH SITA, WHERE ARE you?" cried Hanuman desperately. "I've searched every room in every building, and in every nook and cranny in Lanka, and yet still you evade me. Are you in a deep dungeon I know not where, or have you died of grief. Has Ravan committed the most heinous crime and ended your life? Oh Sita, where can you be?"

Hanuman went on searching in this frame of mind, often nearly weeping at the thought of what might have happened to the Princess.

"I cannot return without some news of Sita, good or bad," he lamented.

With that, Hanuman turned a corner as the first streaks of dawn appeared on the eastern horizon, and flew down a narrow path leading to a grove of trees lined with fountains, an ashoka grove he was certain he had never seen before.

It was a heavily secluded ornamental garden, replete with flowers and terraces, decorated with precious metals, crystals and corals. Little bells suspended from the trees tinkled in the breeze. Not a leaf was out of place, the fountains and ponds sparkling and clear, with ornamental fish swimming contentedly within. Definitely, it was a special place.

"Oh Lord Vishnu," prayed Hanuman, "please let Sita be here. Ram told me how fond she was of gardens. Surely there is a chance she might be close by."

Approaching a fountain in the center of the park, its white marble shining in the early morning light, he heard a whimpering sound. As he neared, he saw five very ugly guards sitting on the grass. Some had bent noses; others had missing teeth. One was completely bald with a face like a rat. All carried spears.

Off to one side, sat on the ground under a large tree, was a beautiful woman dressed in a crumpled yellow sari. She was crying. Her long dark hair, tied in a single strand, hung down her back, and in the half—light, Hanuman saw she was thin and pale.

"That must be Sita!" he said, quivering in anticipation.

Hanuman wanted to get closer, so changed to his normal size, flew up into a tree, and hearing a cry, climbed down through the branches until he saw her clearly. At that moment, the lady turned her head, and Hanuman gazed directly into the face of Sita.

How beautiful she was, he thought. Even after being held against her will in this inhospitable place, for so many days and nights, separated from the man she loves, she still looked so pure and gentle, flawless and divine. It was no wonder that, for her, demons Khara and Dushana, and fourteen thousand rakshas warriors had met their grisly end. But before he could act, a procession entered the garden, making its way directly towards them. At its head, dressed in white, gloriously adorned with jeweled crown and golden bracelets, shoulders as broad as a mountain plateau, was the King of Lanka, accompanied by a dozen women carrying torches and waving chamara fans.

"That must be Ravan, come to harm Sita, or even to kill her," growled Hanuman.

His breathing became long and deep, as he prepared to pounce, ready to kill, if need be.

"Sita, you're so beautiful when you cry," the demon said as the procession stopped in front of her. "Do not fear. I have not come to harm you. Trust me. I just want your love. Give it, and it will be returned a thousand fold. Surrender, and you will enjoy immense riches and everlasting happiness."

"You cannot possess me." Sita told him wearily. "I belong to Ram."

"Sweet Princess, you have plenty of time," said Ravan, taking a step towards her. "Just let your love for me flow. You will find it quite natural."

"Do not approach me, you - you monster," she said, as she picked up a straw and placed it between them on the ground.

"As you wish, but your beloved Ram cannot save you. Lanka is impenetrable, and my forces have never known defeat. I shall give you one week. If you do not surrender to me by then, you will die. Guards, take very good care of my prize," he barked, scaring the birds out of the trees.

The demon king swung round, cape flying like a large butterfly, and strode arrogantly off through the trembling guards.

"Out of my way, fools," he shouted. "Bend her to my will if you value your lives!"

After Ravan had gone, Trijata, the head ogre, came forward.

"O charming one, withdraw your mind from Ram. Take Ravan as your husband. You will make a fine, devoted wife. But be quick. Our lord can be impatient. I think you understand."

An ogress with one ear, pushed in front.

"Stupid woman!" she hissed. "You had better to do so. Many things unpleasant happen to those who displease our master!"

Then an ogre with a broken nose stepped forward. "Wretch! No one defies our master and lives. If you do not submit you will die. They all have. Ha! Ha! Ha!"

Another ogress jumped onto the fountain.

"Ooohh, yes!" she shrilled. "Let me nibble her flesh. Yummy, yummy, yummy!"

A fifth ogress barged her way to the front.

"No! I'm first!"

When the last three ogres pounced on Sita, Trijata dragged them off.

"Stop! Idiots!" she cried. "There is not one good brain among you. She has to be kept alive!"

"Dolt heads, you!" snarled the one-eared ogress.

Meanwhile, Sita curled up in a pathetic little ball, and rocked back and forth, sobbing softly.

"Let us leave her to think things over," spat Trijata. "I'm sure she will make the right decision."

When the guards were gone, Hanuman, who had heard everything, felt close to tears to see poor Sita suffer so. Now she was alone, he had a chance to talk to her, maybe bring some comfort. But how was he to communicate? If he suddenly appeared in front of her, monkey that he was, she would certainly take fright.

And then an idea came to him, and assuming his most melodious voice, broke the pre-dawn silence in the garden by saying. "King Dasarath had four righteous sons. The eldest, Ram, a great warrior, married the beautiful Princess Sita. But one day, a terrible demon stole her, and took her across the sea to his island fortress. Ram, filled with fathomless grief for his lost Princess, sent a messenger to find her."

Sita stopped crying and stood up. At that moment, Hanuman jumped down in front of her, and she stepped back in astonishment.

"Oh, dear," said Hanuman. "I'm sorry, my lady, it was not my intent to frighten you. I'm a friend. I mean you no harm."

"What sort of friend could you be?" gasped Sita.

"I've been sent by King Sugriva himself, to find you."

"Who? I've never heard of him. For all I know, you could be a spy for the monster who keeps me prisoner here."

"No, I'm a messenger on a noble errant," he told her. "My name is Hanuman," and taking out Ram's signet ring, he gave it to her.

Sita inspected it closely.

"This is Ram's ring!" she exclaimed. "So you must be Ram's messenger. Oh, Hanuman, please warn my husband that Ravan has given me one week to live!"

"Have faith, my lady. Ravan will be thwarted in his evil designs on you."

"But where is Ram? Why did he not come?"

"There's a great plan afoot to free you, my lady," he told her. "As I speak, thousands of brave warriors prepare to march on Lanka. Now that I've found you, I must inform Ram."

At that, Sita broke down in tears.

"Please do not cry, my lady," Hanuman begged her. "Ram is heartbroken, and misses you so much. Now, before we are seen talking together, it is time for me to go."

"Wait!" Sita said, unpinning the crest jewel from her hair. "Please give this to Ram. Tell him to come quickly."

"I will," he promised her, "but first I must take some revenge on Ravan for what he has done to you."

And with that he flew off to destroy Ravan's favorite garden.

"Oh, Hanuman, be careful," Sita cried, as he launched himself up and disappeared.

Hanuman went through the ashoka grove, felled all the beautiful trees and threw them in the ponds. He uprooted the shrubs and bushes and tossed them in the tanks. He trampled the flowers and smashed the rockeries and ornamental fountains, and broke all the pots and statues.

It was over quite quickly, but Hanuman made such a noise, the guards were alerted. But by the time they had arrived, he had disappeared.

Ravan was filled with fury when he heard his favorite garden had been destroyed.

"Bring the one responsible to me," he roared at his commanders. "Whoever he is, he has not long to live."

Hanuman heard the bugles and drums, saw the advancing army, and prepared to fight. A detachment of soldiers, led by Ravan's son, Prince Aksa, arrived at the gate, as more soldiers scrambled over the wall.

"I'm over here," Hanuman cried, "Come and get me!"

The troops opened fire, but Hanuman's thick hide deflected their arrows. Picking up a handful of warriors, he dashed them to the ground. Grabbing a pillar, he swung it around his head, decimating a dozen more.

And in return, Aksa pulled out three arrows, and incensed Hanuman by striking him on the forehead, whereupon Hanuman emitted red-hot rays from his smoldering eyes, burning Aksa and those who stood nearby. Then he grabbed Aksa by the ankles and dashed him to the ground.

When news reached Ravan of the death of one of his sons and the destruction of his force, he turned to his eldest, Indrajit.

"Take a division and bring me the person responsible," his father roared. "Alive!"

When they returned with a larger force, Hanuman surprised them by pretending to be fearful, and refused to fight, knowing full well that this was the only way he could meet Ravan and obtain any extra vital information.

When Indrajit saw the extent of the destruction, and the tattered remains of the rakshas army, he immediately let fly an arrow at Hanuman, binding him so tight, he could not move. Hanuman gave up, and was led away. After the troops had left, it became very still in the garden, the only sound the waterfall, tinkling and plopping into the blood red pond.

CHAPTER 34

DESTRUCTION IN LANKA

HANUMAN WAS DRAGGED INTO the throne room, past crowds of screaming demons, and stood before Ravan. The demon king's black body shimmered in the reflection of thousands of jewels located around the room.

Hanuman eyed him contemptuously.

"On your knees, wretch!" spat a guard.

"Father, this is the one who killed Prince Aksa, and destroyed the ashoka grove, annihilating our entire force," roared Indrajit.

"Who are you, vile creature?" demanded Ravan, scathed to the core. "Which god sent you? Be quick. Your time is short!"

"My name is Hanuman," he replied coolly. "The destruction of the garden was a ruse to enable me to meet you. It was a pity so many of your men had to die. So many pretty flowers got trampled as well."

Ravan rose from his throne, eyes burning, as Indrajit came toward Hanuman, whip in hand.

"Less of your impertinence!" he snapped, cracking Hanuman across the back. "Father, let me teach this chimp a lesson."

"I shall deal with him," Ravan said gravely, as he marched over to Hanuman, looking like death. "What is your business in Lanka?"

"I come with a message from my master," Hanuman told him, staring boldly at the king as he approached.

"So you're a courier," said Ravan, staring contemptuously at Hanuman. "Then give us your message quickly. You won't be alive much longer."

"You keep my master's wife against her will, in the ashoka," Hanuman accused him.

"You are very observant," Ravan said.

"I have been authorized by Prince Ram and King Sugriva to find her."

"Prince Ram? Well, well!"

"To abduct someone's wife is a great sin," Hanuman reminded him, "Let Sita go and no further action will be taken against you. Keep her here, and each one of you will pay the ultimate price."

"Brave words from a mere monkey," Ravan scoffed.

"You don't have to be brave to steal someone's wife!" Hanuman retorted.

"You impudent ape!"

"Sita is wasting away in your company," shouted Hanuman. "Reunite her with her husband and you will be saved. Khara, Dushana, and their whole army have already been defeated. Why risk your entire city for one woman?"

"Enough of this! For your insolence you will die. Guards! Take him away!"

The soldiers dragged Hanuman across the floor as Ravan's brother, Vibhishan, a tall, slim warrior, with a gracious air, appeared.

"Dear brother, to kill an envoy goes against all codes of conduct. He can be whipped, branded or mutilated…"

"Vibhishan, keep out of this!" Indrajit snarled venomously.

"Don't tell me what I can or cannot do, brother," Ravan said. "He has killed my son. He must die."

He's a messenger," argued Vibhishan, sent by others. "They are the real enemy. Better to direct an attack on them. Send him away with a message of our own."

Ravan glared at Vibhishan for a long time. No one dared breathe. Somehow managing to control his wrath, Ravan turned, puffing and fuming to the guards restraining Hanuman, as Ministers and courtiers stared at each other in disbelief, knowing Vibhishan would certainly have died right there and then, had he not been Ravan's brother.

"Yes, Vibhishan, you are right. I was being too hasty. To kill a messenger goes against all moral codes. Mmmmm, I'm led to believe a monkey's tail is very dear to him. Let us test this out. Guards! Set fire to his tail then let him go!"

Hanuman jumped about frantically as a rag was wound around his tail. He had not expected this. A soldier, eager to obey his master, brought a torch. Hanuman squirmed and chattered, then swished his tail, knocking over three guards.

"Hold him tight!" shouted Indrajit.

More guards jumped on Hanuman, pining him down, and he struggled no more, putting on a brave face as a blazing torch was brought down on his tail, setting it alight.

"Go tell your Ram, I will never give up Sita!" shouted Ravan.

The guards carefully escorted him outside, leading him through the streets as an act of humiliation, but the brave Hanuman was more concerned about what he had to accomplish in Lanka, and saw the city once more, this time in daylight, and made good use of the opportunity to get a layout of the streets.

As his tail started to blaze, Hanuman turned to look at it, and decided it was time to go. He meditated on a special mantra, the ropes slackened off, and he made his escape. Leaping high in the air, he let out a tremendous war cry, and flew off, while rakshas guards stood open-mouthed.

"Stop him, you fools!" screamed Ravan, as Hanuman flew over them, straight to the nearest house of gold with its thatched roof. Reasoning it would be a good idea to inflict as much damage to Lanka as he could, he touched his blazing tail to it. Soon, much to Hanuman's joy, because the adjoining houses were much of the same material, building after building after golden building had caught fire and melted to the ground exposing the gray stonework underneath.

He visited squares and market places, setting stalls and houses alight. The resultant fire roared out of control, forcing people into the streets, hungry flames licking at vestibules and portals, consuming vast areas of the city.

Sita sat under her tree in the ashoka grove, and smelt burning. She stood, and saw smoke rising, heard soldiers running and shouting, and immediately thought of Hanuman. A smile crossed her face for the first time in months.

As Hanuman flew over the Ashoka grove, Sita waved vigorously, and could tell by his victory loop, he was pleased with his work. She watched as he grew to his full size again and soared off through the clouds, knowing he was eager to bring Ram the good news.

CHAPTER 35

VIBHISHAN

As THE SUN SET, Ravan stood in somber mood on a balcony with his brother Vibhishan and ministers, surveying the charred, smoking remains of the city.

"Look at my beautiful city, ruined!" he cried.

"Brother, I want to help you," Vibhishan told him. "Please listen to what I have to say. Sita must be returned to Ram."

An outraged Ravan turned to Vibhishan, his black eyes reflecting the flames of the still burning city.

"You took another man's wife, and that is why Lanka burns," Vibhishan told him, "This is the root cause of all your suffering."

Ravan gave Vibhishan a long, cold stare.

"We come into this world with nothing, yet you want to possess everything," Vibhishan continued. "You must accept the fact that everything is owned and controlled by the Supreme, and that we should only accept those things given to us in this lifetime by higher authority, not what belongs to others."

"Nonsense!"

"You cannot have more than what is allotted you, brother. It you do, you become a thief."

"You forget that I am Ravan, King of the Rakshas," he boasted. "I can have anything I want."

"Brother, everything has a price," Vibhishan reminded him. "There is still time to return Sita. If you do not, you will incur the wrath of the gods."

"The gods tremble at the sound of my name," snapped Ravan.

"Don't you see brother," Vibhishan said, indicating the charred ruins of the city, "you cannot win. This is the price you pay for your uncontrollable lust and your insatiable greed."

"Enough!" Ravan cried.

"You may be a great devotee of Lord Brahma," continued Vibhishan, "and he may have granted you special powers, but if you misuse those powers, brother, you will be defeated."

"You go too far," Ravan hissed so close to Vibhishan that his hot breath burned his cheeks.

"You've brought all this on yourself," continued Vibhishan, undaunted. "Had you not kidnapped Ram's wife, your city would still be intact. Abducting Sita was your biggest mistake."

"You impudent wretch!" Ravan snarled. "Do you think I am afraid of some obscure prince?"

"This prince will come and take his revenge. He will destroy our city. Kill our people. All because you want to enjoy!"

"Traitor!" screamed Ravan, knocking him to the ground, and drawing his sword, pushed the tip against Vibhishan's throat.

"If you were not my brother, I would kill you right now!" he panted. "Now leave Lanka, and never come back!"

CHAPTER 36

THE RETURN OF HANUMAN

Sunlight glinted across the wide expanse of ocean, creating billions of dazzling diamonds, as Hanuman streaked through the sky and made a perfect landing on the beach.

Jambavan was the first to greet him.

"Welcome back, Hanuman," he declared joyfully. "We had given you up. Did you find Sita?"

When Hanuman told him that he had, scores of monkeys surrounded him, dancing for joy. Pressing his palms together and bowing, he accepted their praise.

"Tell us what happened," Angad demanded, tugging at Hanuman's arm.

"Well, I found Sita in an ashoka grove, which turned out to be Ravan's favorite garden. She was safe and well."

"Hurray!" chorused the monkeys.

"But what I saw made me very sad. Her dress was crumpled, and she looked very pale, unhappy being kept prisoner against her wishes. But, when she understood I was on a mission from Ram, I saw hope in her eyes."

Hanuman told them how he destroyed the garden, and was captured by the demons. The monkeys cheered and booed as Hanuman recounted the story, and when he told them of the burning of Lanka, the monkeys became ecstatic.

"We should all go to Lanka and fight these rakshas," yelled Angad. "Hanuman knows the plan of their city and can lead us. We can defeat Ravan and rescue Sita."

"Calm down, Angad," said Jambavan, "Ram gave us clear instructions. We are to find Sita and report. That's all. Now let's return with the good news."

Jambavan looked at Hanuman.

"Ram and Sugriva will be well pleased with you, Hanuman."

The army broke camp and began their long march back to Kishkinda. On their return, the whole city turned out to greet the warriors, lining the streets and balconies, waving flags. The sound of trumpets and music blared out all across the city, and for miles through the forest the joyful fanfare could be heard.

"Welcome back, dear friend," Ram said as Hanuman entered the royal palace. "Did you find my Sita?"

"My Lord," Hanuman replied, bowing. "Sita is safe and well. I located her sitting alone under a tree in the ashoka grove."

"Oh, Hanuman, that's good news. Thank you," said Ram with relief.

"She was overjoyed to be found and gave me this token to bring back to you," he said, handing Ram the brooch.

Ram took the brooch and stroked it affectionately.

"We have less than a week to reach Lanka," said Jambavan. "Ravan says he will permanently deal with Sita then."

"I'm sure we will get there in time, Ram," asserted Lakshman.

"What is your full report?" Sugriva asked as Ram clasped the brooch to his heart.

"Your Majesty, I have the number of Ravan's forces, and his troop displacements."

"Good work, Hanuman," Sugriva said. "For this I'm making you a general. Alert the army. Tomorrow we march on Lanka."

"Congratulations, Hanuman," said Jambavan.

Next day, with the entire monkey army gathered, Ram, flanked by Sugriva, Lakshman, Angad and Jambavan, addressed them.

"Friends, this will be a day to remember. Today, we march on Lanka to defeat the demon king Ravan, rescue Sita, and all those kept against their will. This is a proud time for all monkey warriors, a time about which you will proudly tell your sons and daughters, who, in turn, will tell their children. My brother and I are privileged to serve with you. May all of you be victorious in all your actions."

After roaring their approval, the monkeys loaded stores and munitions onto mules, camels, elephants and horses, checked and distributed arms, and packed up rations. When all was ready, Hanuman formed them up into divisions.

"Prepare to march!" he bellowed in his best generals voice. "Left turn, quick march to Lanka!"

And so the monkey army left Kishkinda and headed for the coast, and the epic adventure that was to come.

CHAPTER 37

THE MARCH ON LANKA

DAY AFTER DAY, THE monkey army battled their way through dark foreboding forest, hacking at vines and branches with their swords until eventually, as bats shrieked overhead, they broke through the last of the jungle undergrowth, and found themselves on the beach.

Lakshman looked worriedly at Ram as they stepped onto the hot sand beneath shady palm trees.

"Ram, what do we do now?" he asked.

Ram looked out to sea, and realized fully, for the first time, what a daunting task it would be to rescue Sita from a fortress city in a faraway land on the other side of an inhospitable ocean. His loss was even sharper now that she was so near yet so far. He remembered how happy they had been in Ayodhya, how he looked into Sita's lotus-like eyes, and caressed her soft face with the back of his hand, how they had walked together through the parks and around the lakes before returning to sit in their sweet smelling garden by the fountain, while above them in the trees the birds sang in never-ending chorus. How distant all that seemed now.

"Have we come thus far only to be beaten by the ocean?" asked Lakshman.

"Sugriva believes that we can make a plan," said Ram. "But now that we are here, I cannot think what it could be. Lakshman, my heart is breaking, and we are running out of time."

"All is not lost, Ram. Let's make camp here and rest. I'm sure we'll find a way to cross."

"I know that time is a great healer, Lakshman, but my agonies increase as time goes on."

"Ram, please don't give up now," Lakshman said gently.

***

Next day, Ram, Sugriva, Jambavan, Angad, Hanuman and Lakshman, met together outside a tent at a makeshift table.

"How do we get the entire army across that ocean?" asked Sugriva. "Does anyone have any ideas? Hanuman, what do you think?"

"I can fly to Lanka on my own, but it would be impossible to carry the entire army across."

"Why don't we build a bridge?" suggested Angad.

"A bridge? Why that would take months, years," said Sugriva.

"Just a small one," suggested Angad.

"A bridge would be a mammoth undertaking," said Jambavan.

"Is there another way across?" Lakshman asked.

"There must be another way," insisted Ram. "There must."

Ram knew there was a way to cross, just as Ravan knew of a way to take Sita, and he wandered along the beach, thinking deeply.

Suddenly, there was a shrill monkey cry from one of the lookouts posted high in a palm tree. "Enemy aircraft!"

"Take defensive positions!" Sugriva shouted as a glowing object appeared from the south, heading in their direction, and came to a halt, hovering in the sky above them.

"It's a rakshas vimana!" Angad shouted, as it began to descend.

The guard assembled on the beach and waited.

"Beware," Sugriva warned as it landed on the soft sand not far from where the army was assembling. "They may be unfriendly."

Troopers had begun to surround the craft from a safe distance, some kneeling with weapons ready, when a panel in the side of the ship slid open, and out stepped Vibhishan, dressed in body armor and helmet, wearing a large sword, followed by four companions.

"We come in peace," he shouted, raising his hands in the air as six monkey warriors came to escort them over to Sugriva. "My name is Vibhishan, and these are my ministers. My brother, Ravan, holds the wife of Prince Ram on Lanka. Ravan has done many evil things, but this has lost him my allegiance for all time. I had no part in his plan to abduct Sita, and offer my sword and surrender."

"Have you seen my Sita?" Ram demanded, striding across the sand towards him.

"She is being well looked after," Vibhishan assured him. "Please, Prince Ram, I wish to help you revenge yourself against my brother and his evil empire."

"Careful," warned Lakshman. "This might be a trick."

"I owe my life to this man," Hanuman said, stepping forward. "He saved me from certain death at the hands of Ravan, and deserves the benefit of any doubt."

"Is this true, Vibhishan?" said Ram.

"I challenged my brother, but he refused to let Sita go, and banished me from Lanka. I come to you with all humility. My only wish is to help you."

"Anyone who surrenders unto me receives my full protection," said Ram. "Vibhishan, you can assist us. You may have useful knowledge we can use to overthrow this demoniac government, and bring peace to the world."

"How large is the force that opposes us?" asked Sugriva.

"Ravan commands a formidable army," said Vibhishan, "he has great generals and even greater weapons. Furthermore, to increase his power, he has been granted protection from Devas, *Gandharvas* and all Celestials. Also, watch out for his son, Indrajit. He misuses the mystic powers without discrimination."

"Ram, my brother shows no mercy," Vibhishan continued, "I will help you any way I can, but you must try to cross the ocean soon, and to do that, you must call on Samudra, God of the Sea. It is the only way. Without his help, you must face defeat."

CHAPTER 38

SAMUDRA, LORD OF THE OCEAN

Ram sat on an outcrop of rock further down the beach and began to meditate, oblivious to the waves crashing around him. All day long, and into the night, he beseeched Samudra to appear, but without success. Ram sat there all the next day, without food or water, and the day after that.

"Samudra, can you hear me?" he finally cried aloud, "I've been calling you for three days and nights. Please help. My wife is in danger. Why don't you answer?"

The breakers began to pound the beach in an ever-increasing roar. But beyond that, although he waited in breathless anticipation, there was no further response. Finally, Ram's patience evaporated, and he stood up, shaking with anger and shouted above the noise of the surf, his eyes glowing like red-hot coals.

"I will vaporize the very ocean if you do not appear!" he cried, taking up his bow.

At that the sea began to boil and froth, generating monster waves that crashed onto the beach, sending sea creatures to the surface.

"Ram, please stop," Lakshman shouted. "Put down your bow!"

But Ram had lost all reason. His anger out of control, he loaded the Brahmastra arrow, aimed at the sky and jerked back the string, whereupon the earth trembled and shook, the sky turned black and the wind increased to gale force. Heavy thunder rolled across the heavens, torches of flame shot down from the sky, trees uprooted, and small animals darted around in fear.

Suddenly, the ocean turned a ghostly shade of green, and erupted, boiling and frothing, whipping up monster waves that crashed all around Ram. As the gale force wind reached a crescendo, Samudra, the Lord of the Ocean, dressed in green silken garments with ornaments of coral and precious gems, and wearing a necklace of pearls, rose majestically out of the water.

"Who has called me from the great depths?" he said, standing on the crest of a wave.

"I have, my lord," said Ram, lowering his bow.

"Who are you, and what do you want?"

"I am Prince Ram of Ayodhya, my lord, and I have called you out of despair. My wife has been kidnapped by the demon Ravan, and is being held captive on an island fortress on Lanka."

"I've heard of this Ravan," Samudra replied. "He is a great demon whose evil exploits are well known throughout the three worlds. You have pleased me with your austerity, Prince Ram. How can I help you?"

"Please allow us to cross your waters to Lanka to rescue my wife."

"By nature, my waters are wide and very deep and cannot be crossed. But, your request is reasonable, and which I grant, because of your high moral character, and the need to return your wife. But, first, you must bridge my straits. Call on Nala, the craftsman within your ranks. He'll build you causeway of rocks and trees. Don't worry Ram, spiritual potency will keep them afloat."

As Samudra slowly submerged again into the ocean, the waves abated, the sea calmed, and the wind dropped.

At first light next day, an assembly line of monkeys formed on the beach, stretching back from the jungle right up to the waters edge. Rocks and trees picked up from the surrounding hills, forest, and along the beach, were handed from monkey to monkey, until they reached the sea, where Nala, a huge monkey whose large hands with hardened palms had completed many a building project, supervised the placement of the first stone by taking a large rock from a monkey and placing it in the water. It immediately sank, and then bobbed to the surface again, floating miraculously, rocking gently on the waves. When Hanuman, flying overhead, dropped a great rock in the water, it sank and rose again to float with the others.

"Now, bring more," said Nala, "a lot more!"

Soon, a strange looking causeway constructed of trees and rocks jutted out into the ocean. Ram, Lakshman and Nala stood admiring it from a hilltop overlooking the beach.

"We seem to be making good time," said Ram.

"Yes," replied Lakshman. "The monkeys are working hard."

"We are about half way across, Prince Ram," said Nala, a few days later. "At this rate the bridge should be finished very soon."

"That is good, Nala. It is heartening to watch them work, and wonderful to think with every stick and stone these monkey warriors place in the water, brings Sita a little closer."

A small bird landed on the causeway and dropped a twig onto the bridge.

"Look, even the little creatures want to help," said Ram.

After more days of hard work, the causeway was, at last, finished, and Ram held a special ceremony on the beach.

"The causeway to Lanka is complete," he said, "thank you for all your help. Tomorrow we march."

The monkeys cheered loudly, and the little bird landed on a tent pole, chirping enthusiastically, but, later that evening, a strong wind started to blow, flapping the tents and obliterating everything with sand.

"There's a big storm approaching, sire," the night guard said on entering Ram's tent.

Ram went to check the bridge, watching it ride the swell. The stones and trees moved up and down with each passing wave, and seemed to be holding together. Lightning flashed on the horizon as loose sand was blown along the beach.

Asking the guard to let him know if there were signs that the bridge was threatened, Ram returned to bed.

During the night, a fierce storm lashed the coast. The wind howled down the beach as the bridge bucked in the huge swell. Giant waves crashed onto it, threatening to smash it to pieces.

Called by the guards, Ram, Lakshman and Sugriva braved the elements to inspect it.

"Its possible the bridge may be destroyed," shouted Sugriva above the howling wind.

"Ram, will it hold?" Lakshman cried.

"It must!" Ram told him, looking anxiously out to sea, his face full of sadness.

The next morning Ram found the bridge battered, but intact. He noticed all the guards had fallen asleep, and looked at them with great compassion.

Ram convened a meeting with Lakshman, Sugriva, Jambavan and Vibhishan to discuss the crossing, and found that they agreed that the bridge was safe to cross.

Ram addressed the troops Sugriva assembled on the beach.

"Today, my friends, we march on Lanka to defeat the demonic forces who are holding Sita captive. All I ask is you fight like you've been trained to, and show no mercy. Prepare to move."

"Battalions, forward march!" Hanuman bellowed, at a sign from Sugriva.

Cheering wildly, the monkey army moved onto the bridge, standard bearers, infantrymen, camels, mules, horses and elephants proceeding slowly towards the isle of Lanka.

It was many hours later when an endless stream of troops trickled onto the beaches of Lanka. Hour after hour, hundreds of thousands of monkey warriors disgorged from the end of the causeway, mustering at their assembly points, filling the beach to capacity.

Thousands of tents sprang up, stretching back across the flat ground behind the beach. Monkeys were still streaming off the causeway as the sun set. As the moon rose, illuminating the landscape with its pale silvery glow, the monkeys lit campfires and sat chattering to each other, while a gentle breeze blew, bringing the sound of kettledrums from the direction of Lanka.

The monkeys gawked at each other in excitement, and then as one, roared back, making such a dreadful sound that the citizens of Lanka looked up in fear and, struck with panic, ran for their homes. Out on the battlements, soldiers stared blankly at each other.

CHAPTER 39

ANGADA

AT DAWN THE NEXT day, Ram gathered his generals and commanders together to plan the attack on Lanka.

"What do you know of Lanka's defenses?" he asked Vibhishan.

" Prince Ram, I sent my spies in to report their positions and defense tactics. Ravan's Commander in Chief, General Prahastha, guards the East Gate, Mahaparshva and Mahodara the South Gate, and Indrajit is in charge of the West Gate. Ravan controls the North Gate, and Virupaksha guards the Central Fortress."

"Good. Neela, you will attack the East Gate. Angad you take the South Gate. Hanuman, take the West. Lakshman and I will take the North."

"Prince Ram," asked a monkey officer, "what do you think the opposition will be like?"

"I am only certain of one thing," Ram replied. "The opposition will be very surprised."

The monkeys knew they would be fighting to uphold dharma, morality, righteousness and justice. Also important, they were defending their religious principles, so were glad to be marching to the rescue of Princess Sita.

That evening, Ram wandered through the monkey ranks, answering questions and putting minds at rest, but when he retired to his tent, his thoughts turned to Sita, held captive, surrounded by demoniac forces, and his heart sank.

***

Before entering into battle, Sugriva decided to send an envoy to Lanka in one final attempt to reach a peaceful solution.

"Angad, I'm sending you to Lanka. I'm giving Ravan one last chance, if he releases Sita, we'll call off our attack. If not, he leaves us no choice."

Angad and a monkey officer made their way into the city hidden in a cart. But once inside the walls, they let themselves be captured.

"So what do we have here," laughed Ravan, "a couple of itinerant monkeys!"

"I come with a message from Prince Ram," Angad said, scowling.

"What does this Prince Ram want?"

"He says, that if you release his wife, your kingdom will be spared."

"This Ram is no threat to me!"

"Ram wants to keep peace and avoid a war, saving many innocent souls," continued Angad. "If you free Sita your city will be spared."

"Ach, this foolish Ram, he thinks he can bargain with the King of the Universe. And if I refuse?"

"You will all die."

"I'm shaking in my shoes," Ravan told him, whereupon, the whole assembly broke down into hysterical fits of laughter.

"It does not pay to fool with Ram!" bellowed Angad.

"It does not pay to fool with me!" Ravan retorted. "Very soon, Sita will be my Queen. But, if she refuses to accept that privileged position; she will be quite dead, and your Prince Ram will never see her again. Lock these two up, and throw away the key." he told the guards.

"You treacherous dog," Angad growled. "You can't lock me up!"

Angad and the monkey officer wrestled free from the guards holding them, knocked two more to the ground, and jumped out a window.

"After them, you fools!" shouted Ravan.

But, battering their way past guards, they made their escape.

"We don't have much time, sire," Angad said upon return. "Ravan says he will kill Sita with his own hands if she doesn't agree to become his Queen. He even tried to imprison us."

Grim faced, Ram summoned his commanders.

"Ravan has decided not to accept our proposal," he told them. "We attack at dawn."

Malyavan, a senior minister to Ravan, decided to offer the Demon King some advice, and stepped up to the throne.

"Your majesty, I beg you to reconsider. It would be wise to return Sita, before it is too late. The boons you were granted by Lord Brahma do not give you full protection."

Ravan looked squarely at Malyavan.

"An exiled Prince, with a bunch of monkeys, threatens me with war, and you have the gall to demand I surrender? Get out of my sight!"

CHAPTER 40

THE BATTLE FOR LANKA

As THE SUN ROSE the next day, the monkey army made its way across the hills and onto the plains of Lanka. Ram positioned them near the city, yet beyond the range of any missiles, after which Ram, Lakshman, Sugriva, Jambavan and Hanuman moved to the forefront of the troops and waited. A gentle breeze rippled through the grass. A horse snorted. A bridle clinked.

"May Lord Vishnu protect us," Ram began, facing the ranks, only to be interrupted by Vibhishan and an aide arriving from Lanka.

"I bring bad news," Vibhishan told him. "My spies tell me Ravan has given Sita two hours to live. We returned as fast as we could."

"Lakshman, we have less time than we think," Ram cried.

"That is not all, sire," added Vibhishan, "Ravan has brought in reinforcements. He now outnumbers us two to one, and the main gates have been strengthened!"

"We attack immediately!" Ram shouted.

Ram dropped his arm.

A thousand trumpets, bugles, drums, conches and cymbals shattered the morning air, as the army surged forward, a chanting, yelling, pulsating body of highly motivated monkey warriors. The noise was deafening. The monkey army, eager to see action yelled and beat their shields as they charged towards the city, many arming themselves with trees and boulders as they went.

On the battlements of Lanka, a sleepy guard was startled into wakefulness by the sound of drums and cymbals, and saw, coming up the hill, stretching as far as the eye could see, an immense army of monkeys! An instant later, a rock knocked him out cold.

One panicking soldier ran in the direction of the Royal palace. He burst into the throne room, pointing frantically towards the city wall.

"Your Majesty! Armies of monkeys are attacking from the West and the North. They are everywhere!"

From the balcony Ravan saw for himself, the monkey army surging across the plain towards the main gates, as his soldiers sprinted to their positions.

"Open fire!" he bellowed across the battlements.

As arrows screamed down from the city walls, ripping into the monkeys, many died instantly. Ram and Lakshman returned fire, and thunderbolts flew over the city walls, exploding in the courtyard.

"Launch the Vimanas! Attack! Attack!" Ravan shouted to his Commander-in-Chief, General Prahastha.

The city gates burst open, pouring out hordes of demon cavalry, followed by chariots and infantry.

The monkeys lunged forward, clashing head on with Ravan's infantry. Man met man, and demon met monkey.

Rakshas vimanas flew over the city, firing down on the army, killing many.

Lakshman dived for cover, joining Ram behind a rock.

"We're being decimated," shouted Lakshman. "What do we do?"

Ram watched as demons riding on beasts plunged into battle, monkeys mounted on elephants and horses facing them, and saw the ground gradually turn red.

"Back! Get everyone back!" shouted Ram.

When the monkeys fell back and took cover, Ram directed a new attack from another direction and the army moved forward again. But as monkey casualties increased, and another attack sent them under cover again, Ram took shelter behind a felled tree, and for the first time, considered the possibility of a defeat.

Another explosion threw dirt and debris over their position. As Lakshman rolled against Ram, he saw a sparkle of light run down his sword.

"Ram, we must use the mystical weapons," he shouted.

Ram called for their armor, and the brothers fired their arrows at the enemy on the walls, blowing out huge chunks of masonry, and killing many rakshas.

At the same time, the monkeys let loose a rain of stones, felling many demons, and then began filling in the moat in front of each gate with mud, rocks and trees, while Ram and Lakshman fired arrows at super speed, knocking demons off their mounts, the twang of Ram's powerful bow ringing above the noise of battle.

Monkeys speared serpents, as rakshas ran for cover, some crushed by their dying mounts.

Shape-shifter demons appeared and disappeared, changing their hideous forms at every moment. Vibhishan moved forward, and fired arrows at the shape shifters, forcing them back.

Meanwhile, vimanas roared overhead, unloading laser ray weapons into the army, obliterating many brave monkeys.

Hanuman appeared, fighting half a dozen demons, after felling them all, he picked up a huge boulder and flung it, crushing a general.

The vimanas continued to pose a major problem, and Lakshman fired on the underbelly of one as it passed. Having no effect, he loaded a special arrow and chanted a mantra. This time the weapon blasted a hole in its side, and it crashed into the ground.

Ravan looked up from his chart table as General Prahastha marched in.

"Your Majesty," he announced, "General Dhumraksa has been killed."

"What!" he yelled, hands twitching in anxious frustration.

"Their army is very strong," said Prahastha.

"Nonsense!" retorted Ravan, hammering the table with his fist hard enough to smash it to pieces. "You're going soft on me, General! They're just a puny bunch of monkeys. Increase the guard on the main gates. Keep attacking! Keep attacking!"

Vimanas continued bombing the monkeys, spreading death and destruction among their ranks, while Ram and Lakshman attacked the walls, killing many of the demon army. But when the rakshas launched another massive attack, they were forced to take cover behind a low wall.

They advanced, launching a series of rapid-fire arrows, and although they met terrific resistance, managed to fight their way towards the North Gate, where Ram sent off such a barrage of arrows, that the gate was blown off its hinges. Angad threw a spear at a general, killing him as monkeys stormed through the gate, while Hanuman fought his way into the demon ranks and went after another general, dispatching him with a blow from his mace.

Back at the palace, General Prahastha ran into the throne room in a panic.

"Your Majesty," he cried, "they've breached the North gate and General Vajradamshtra and General Akampan are dead!"

"What, two more Generals? I don't believe it!" Ravan snarled; his voice chillingly distorted. "Bring me my armor. Now! I'll fight them myself!"

Ravan watched his troops beat the monkey army back to the unhinged main gate as he was helped into his armor. Indrajit arrived, and they surveyed the scene together.

"Let me lead the attack, father," he begged only to be ignored as, leaning out the window, Ravan bellowed down to the courtyard. "Prepare my chariot!" Then, turning to General Prahastha, he told him to return to the battlefield and lead the attack.

In the courtyard, Ravan pushed a weird assortment of subhuman warriors out of the way as he strode towards a large set of double doors which, swinging open, revealed a magnificent black war chariot. Mounting it, Ravan rode it to the open North Gate with General Prahastha, leading the Rakshas army, following.

Seeing Lakshman, Ravan fired an astra, knocking the prince to the ground, and then, as he tried to regain his feet, shot a second bolt, blasting off his protective armor, sending him reeling for cover.

General Prahastha attacked with his warriors, and met with fierce opposition from the monkeys led by General Neela, who threw a great boulder at Prahastha, crushing him.

Ram saw a giant of a man driving a black chariot straight toward him, and loaded an arrow, knowing instinctively that it was the devil that had taken his Sita.

His jaw set firmly, Ram checked his bow, took careful aim, and loosened one, which shrieked past Ravan's chariot, burning the pennant to ashes.

"Ha! That must be the Prince!" he snarled, and turned to fire his arrows at Ram.

Ram dodged and weaved as the astras exploded around him, demolishing walls and buildings. The second time Ravan fired at Ram, narrowly missing him, Ram replied with an arrow that scored a direct hit on the chariot. Extracting himself from the wreckage, Ravan found himself face to face with Ram who fired another, which blasted off Ravan's armor, before firing again, neatly splitting Ravan's crown in two.

Hurt and humiliated, his crown smoking, his armor dented, Ravan beat a hasty retreat through the main gate. To stop further attacks and make essential repairs, more rakshas forces appeared and forced the monkeys back.

Ravan burst into the throne room, burnt and twisted armor hanging off him, crying; "I want every available man, demon, reptile, whatever, out on the battlefield, now!"

Soldiers scurried around in confusion as Ravan disappeared down a back stairway and made his way to a small prayer room, kneeling in front of his deity, armor still smoldering.

"Lord Brahma," he prayed, "you have already fulfilled my desire for immeasurable power and immunity from Devas, *Danavas*, Gandharvas and *Yaksas*. Now, grant me victory in battle against this Ram."

"This monkey army is too powerful," complained a captain as Ravan re-entered the throne room.

"This Ramachandra is no match for us," stated another.

Grabbing a senior officer by the lapel, Ravan dragged him to a table where he pointed to a map of the city, his finger stabbing the parchment.

"I want reinforcements here, here and here!" he shouted. "Get men from the kitchens if need be. If we don't repel these cretins, you will die a slow death!"

"Yes, Your Majesty," said the general, looking wide-eyed at Ravan. "But I think we may have underestimated the power of this monkey army."

"Nonsense! As long as I am alive we will win this war. Now get out of my sight and send me someone with brains! The victory is ours!"

CHAPTER 41

THE GIANT

A stocky captain, with bent nose and large ears, and the look of many battles about him, appeared, snapped to attention and saluted, then stood next to Ravan beside the chart table. Ravan took hold of his ear and gave it a twist. "Listen carefully," he grated.

The captain's eyeballs rotated in Ravan's direction, as he gave him his full attention.

"Those damned monkeys have damaged our North Gate. Right?"

"Yes, Your Majesty."

"They have also very active in our Western sector. Right?"

"Yes, Your Majesty."

"And they have also been killing a lot of our men. Right?"

The captain looked a little puzzled.

"Yes, Your Majesty."

"Now, tell me, my friend. What do we do?"

"We need reinforcements, Your Majesty," he said.

Ravan pulled out a dagger and stuck it against the captain's throat.

"You've spent years on the battlefield, Captain. Now tell me. Precisely who?"

The petrified captain's mouth opened, but no sound emerged.

"I'll give you a clue," Ravan snarled, "He's big, and sleeps to gain immortality."

"Kumbakarn!" he exclaimed in a flash of inspiration.

"Wake him!" spat Ravan, screwing up his face in disgust as he threw him out of the room.

"Pull half a dozen men," the captain told a soldier standing nearby as he picked himself up. "We wake the giant."

Ten minutes later, the captain led the way into a huge, dank, musty dungeon. At the end of a long, dark passageway, as he pushed the creaking door open, a blast of stale air rushed at them. The rusty hinges grated as the door was pushed further open to reveal a void. As they entered, loaded with plates of food, drink, sweet smelling flowers, cymbals and drums, their torches spread the light around the room, and they saw the snoring monolithic form of Kumbakarn.

Kumbakarn, a fierce warrior, twenty stories tall, and a demon by trade, was an ugly brute. He lay on a bed of straw, his great feet pressed up against one wall, his matted locks brushing the other.

"All right," the captain said to two of the soldiers. "You and you. Go wake him."

The frightened pair, one carrying a bugle, the other a drum, quietly crept towards the giant, looking at each other in terror.

"You're trying to wake him you fools!" the captain bellowed.

Immediately, the pair started banging the drum, shouting and blowing the bugle. But Kumbakarn slept on. The captain ordered four more guards to shout, clash cymbals and poke the giant with their spears. But still he remained fast asleep.

"Shout in his ear, you idiots!" the captain told them, standing well aside himself.

One soldier climbed onto the mattress and bellowed into Kumbakarn's ear. Some pulled his hair and bit his ears. Still the giant slept on.

"Put torches under his feet! Play those drums! Bring food!"

Two soldiers rushed forward with trays of animal carcasses and flagons of wine, and placed them near the giant's nostrils.

"Now everyone yell!"

The soldiers shouted, yelled, crashed cymbals and beat drums, and after a few moments of this terrific din, the giant slowly began to stir, and opened his eyes, letting out a blood-curdling yell that rocked the foundations of the building. Then throwing his arms wide, he squashed two of the soldiers like flies.

"Who has dared wake me?" Kumbakarn roared, sitting up.

"The city is under attack," the captain shouted. "Ravan needs you on the battlefield right away. Get up and fight."

"Have I been robbed of my immortality because of some petty war?" the giant demanded.

"This is no ordinary war," replied the captain. "The survival of the kingdom depends on you."

Kumbakarn produced a gigantic yawn, gulped down the food and drink, drenching soldiers in wine in the process and rose to his feet. Stretching and burping, he picked up a massive club lying nearby, and dragged himself up the stone steps.

Meanwhile, on the battlefield, the war raged on. The monkey army was getting the upper hand, advancing towards the city gates, when the earth shook, and Kumbakarn appeared. Roaring like an approaching cyclone, he stepped right over the city wall.

The ground trembled and the giant marched across the battlefield, smashing everything in his path, soldiers, and monkeys, even demons. Monkey archers fired volley after volley of arrows, but to no effect. Ignoring them, the monster continued onward, grabbing handfuls of monkeys and demons, eating some, discarding others.

"By the gods, what is that?" Lakshman exclaimed.

"It's Ravan's brother, Kumbakarn," replied Vibhishan.

The monkeys took one look and ran, but some were squashed under the giant's feet.

"Retreat!" Vibhishan cried.

Just then, a giant Hanuman appeared. Kumbakarn turned and growled, and moved towards him, but Hanuman stood his ground.

Ram looked on helplessly, unable to intervene, and reluctantly let Hanuman meet his match.

The giants advanced slowly, eyeing each other. A golden mace appeared in Hanuman's hand, and Kumbakarn raised his huge club, swinging it around his head. The battle of the giants began. They closed, weapons meeting in a flash of light and a mighty crash. They sparred, neither giving an inch. After a few minutes of heavy fighting, Hanuman went down on one knee to catch his breath. Kumbakarn immediately responded with a vicious swing, smashing Hanuman on the shoulder. Rolling over and over in the dust, Hanuman lay still for a moment, and then slowly got to his feet. The giant, urged on by the demons, raised his club once more and brought it crashing down, knocking Hanuman sideways into the city wall. Kumbakarn moved in for the kill, raising his club high above his head, and then...

Whoosh!

An arrow flashed across the battlefield, blasting the club from Kumbakarn's hand. The giant turned, and saw Ram load another.

Uprooting a nearby tree, Kumbakarn heaved it at the prince, and then picked up his club. Ram sidestepped, pulling back his bowstring.

Whoosh!

Another arrow ripped into Kumbakarn's left shoulder, dismembering his arm, still gripping the club, from his gigantic body. Roaring like a volcano, he picked up a boulder just as Ram fired again.

Whoosh!

An astra raced through the air, ripping Kumbakarn's right arm off. Screaming in agony, with renewed fury, the giant rushed at Ram, only to have the fourth arrow sever his right leg from his body. Monkeys scrambled for safety and rakshas dove for cover as the giant began to topple. But, Ram, still bent on destruction, blasted the other leg off. This was the end for Kumbakarn, and he fell. Unfortunately, a few of Ravan's best, who were standing nearby, supplied the softest landing the falling megalith could ever hope for as the torso hit the ground with the force of an earthquake.

All fighting stopped.

After the dust settled, Ram, Vibhishan, Sugriva and Lakshman approached the giant's shattered body.

"He was one of the bravest," said Vibhishan sadly.

"I took no joy in killing your brother," Ram told him. "It was his destiny to die by my hand."

"Do not lament, Vibhishan," said Sugriva, "by Ram's hand, Kumbakarn gained his immortality."

CHAPTER 42

INDRAJIT

MEANWHILE, INDRAJIT AND QUEEN Mandodari, along with Ravan eagerly awaited news in the throne room.

"Your Highness. Kumbakarn has been killed," gasped the first guard to arrive.

"My Kumbakarn! Nooo, it can't be," Ravan cried.

"Who has done this?" Indrajit demanded.

"It was Ramachandra," a second guard shouted.

"Double the guards on the main gates and in the Ashok grove!" ordered a stunned Ravan.

Indrajit snapped his fingers and immediately an aide brought a suit of armor and a pair of special gloves.

"Father, how many more of our brave warriors must die before you come to your senses?" he shouted, pulling on a glove. "Let me bring you Ram's head!"

"I won't risk your life," his father bellowed, face black with rage, thumping the throne with his fists.

"Father, he must be destroyed!" Indrajit retorted. "What is my life worth if I cannot prove myself? I have been trained from birth to protect the dynasty!"

"No!"

"Father, I shall return victorious. This I promise. My name will be celebrated throughout the land."

"Indrajit, you are headstrong and reckless."

"Father, don't treat me like this!" he screamed.

"Please Indrajit," his mother begged him, rising and stretching out her arms. "Don't try to be a hero."

"Father, I can outwit this Ram with my mystic powers," Indrajit said, pushing her away. "Just give me a chance."

Ravan paced the floor, thinking hard.

"Very well, my son," he said finally. "But only on the condition that you perform the sacrifice of immortality."

Turning on his heel, Indrajit strode off, pulling on his armor, shouting orders at the top of his voice. Tears slid down Mandodari's cheeks as she watched from the balcony as he went to the giant temple cave of Nikumbila, knowing that he meant to order the priest who would be chanting mantras within to light the fire and start the sacrifice.

On the battlefield, the fighting continued. Two identical warriors, Kumba and Nikumba, sons of Kumbakarn, fought their way through the monkey ranks towards Sugriva and Hanuman. Arrogant and overconfident, they attacked the two *Varanas*, and were mercilessly cut down.

Indrajit witnessed their demise from his chariot, to which a silver and black projectile had been attached, and his anger rose.

"Now is the time to test the *Nagapasa* missile," he said to himself, thundering over the battlefield. After firing arrows down on the monkeys, and attracting return fire, Indrajit pushed a button on a console, activating an invisibility cloak, and swooping down, fired at Lakshman, forcing him to dodge behind an upturned chariot, after which he fired at Ram, laughing loudly as the Prince tried to avoid the exploding astras.

Then executing a wide turn, with Lakshman in his sights, Indrajit fired the missile. It blasted a large hole in the ground, blowing fifty monkeys across the battlefield, and knocked Lakshman into a death-like trance. Panic immediately swept through the monkey ranks.

"Jambavan, we must do something," Ram cried, clearly desperate, "Lakshman and the monkeys are barely alive. Carry them back to their tents and have a twenty-four watch put on them."

CHAPTER 43

THE HERBS

NIGHT FELL QUICKLY, BRINGING an end to hostilities and relief to the battle worn monkeys. They returned to their tents beside which campfires cast their friendly glow in the alien darkness, most now containing the injured or dying tended by the medical corps. Inside one lay Lakshman, unconscious.

"He's in a bad way," General Sushena, the monkey physician told Ram, who, together with Vibhishan and Sugriva, stood beside his cot. "If we don't do something soon, they may all die. I can think of only one remedy. If we can get to the healing herbs in the mountains."

"Yes, I remember an old sage once talked about a great battle," said Sugriva, "resulting in many wounded. The cure came from herbs growing in the Himalayas. Magic healing herbs; yes, that's what he said, herbs with special properties to cure all ills. It seems like it's the only way."

"Who among you knows the location?" asked Sushena.

"Accha! Hanuman Ji," Jambavan replied. "Let him be called."

"We have a crisis," Ram said, when Hanuman joined them. "Lakshman lies in a coma, and a great number of the monkey warriors have sustained terrible wounds. Their only hope is the healing herbs. You must go to the Mahodaya Mountain in the Himalayas and bring back the Visalyakarani and Samdhini herbs located on its southern slope. Leave immediately!"

Hanuman pressed his palms together. "You can rely on me," he said.

"Be quick! Now, go!" Sugriva told him.

Only a handful of soldiers saw the streak of light in the sky heading northwards. Fewer still knew it was Hanuman, and none knew if the mission would be successful.

Hanuman soared through blizzards, rain and sleet until, eventually, the snowcapped peaks of the Himalayas came into view, shining brilliantly against an azure sky.

It was so cold that Hanuman was soon covered in a thin sheet of ice, but he scarcely noticed, so intent was he on his mission. Flying through a cloud layer, he descended rapidly onto a meadow where the herbs flourished, but as he sought them, they hid from him, until he understood that there was only one thing left for him to do.

***

As the sun rose, Hanuman flew in over Lanka and was spotted by the duty guard.

"Look, it's Hanuman!" he shouted.

"What's that he's carrying?" asked another monkey, as Hanuman made a wobbly but successful landing. And there on the hot barren plains of Lanka, sat a mammoth chunk of Himalayan mountaintop, complete with snow, pine trees, wild flowers and small animals, as if it had literally dropped out of the sky.

"He's brought the whole mountain," cried an astonished Sugriva as his monkey followers climbed onto the peak to collect the herbs to give them to Lakshman and the injured monkeys.

"Now, only time will tell," he said gravely.

Hours passed before Ram was called to his brothers tent to find him conscious. Lakshman opened his eyes and managed to force a smile.

"You have Hanuman to thank," said Ram, as the noble monkey looked inside the tent. "He flew all the way to the Himalayas to fetch the healing herbs."

" Thank you, Hanuman," said Lakshman, "you're the most noble, courageous warrior I've ever known."

CHAPTER 44

INDRAJIT'S DEADLY LESSON

INDRAJIT HAD FLOWN FOR hours, and now, many miles from Lanka, landed beside a small hut half hidden under a stand of trees. Kicking open the door, he stormed inside Marichi's apothecary and began smashing apparatus and upturning tables.

After destroying anything that was not nailed down, he crossed to a bookshelf tucked in a corner, and after quickly checking the shelves, hurled the books on the floor. But only when he jerked a cupboard off the wall did he reveal a hidden compartment containing the large volume which he had come so far to search for, the book that contained the key to the victory he had promised his father.

The next morning, surrounded by infantry, Indrajit drove a chariot, pulled by three white horses, towards Lanka's main gate, holding Sita, hair tangled, and wearing a soiled yellow sari, in front of him. He lashed the horses with a whip, and when they entered the battlefield he drew to a halt, directly in front of Lakshman, Hanuman, and Ram who, dropping his bow, cried out Sita's name.

"Now it's your turn to watch as a loved one dies," Indrajit called out, yanking Sita up by the hair and unsheathing his sword. "You decimated my family, Ramachandra. Now, it's your turn to pay!"

Hanuman stood spellbound, looking at Sita's sad face, remembering the time when he first saw her in the ashoka grove, if only he had grabbed her then. As he rushed forward, Indrajit plunged his sword into Sita's bosom in one easy movement, and she slumped to the floor of the chariot.

"Sitaaaaa!" screamed Ram, arms outstretched.

"Now taste my arrows!" Indrajit shouted, firing at Ram and missing, only to fire again and killing two monkey guards who stood nearby. Shocked, Ram sank to his knees, his head cradled in his hands, crying his beloved's name.

"Let that be a lesson to you all," Indrajit yelled, before re-entering the city.

"This cannot be happening," Lakshman told his brother. "Do not trust your eyes. Do not trust your senses."

"There is something wrong," said Vibhishan. "Ravan would never allow Sita to be killed. It must be a trick. As a child, Indrajit was always pulling tricks."

Sugriva pondered deeply, "Surely you are right," he said. "Ravan would not do such a thing, as long as he stood a chance of winning Sita."

"Indrajit was seen entering the big temple," a monkey sergeant reported.

"Nikumbila!" said Vibhishan quickly. "The sacrifice of immortality! The one who disturbs the yajna can kill him. Come with me, Lakshman!"

Lakshman and Vibhishan sprinted for the temple accompanied by a handful of monkeys.

The temple cave of Nikumbila, an ancient shrine, that once reverberated with the chants of the gods, now stood in ruins, inhabited only by armies of mice, running along its dusty floors, its subterranean passages populated with rat like creatures.

Inside the temple, in a chamber the size of a cathedral, a large fire roared in a massive stone grate, giving the place an eerie glow.

Lakshman and the monkeys entered through a small opening at the rear, and saw Indrajit kneeling. His prayer for immortality and victory over Ram vibrated round the room. Lakshman noticed a missile sitting in a glass case close by, its console lights blinking on and off, and nudged Vibhishan toward it. Hearing them approach, Indrajit stopped in mid prayer, spinning in a rage.

"So you can't give me a moment's peace!" he hissed, his red eyes blazing.

Indrajit grabbed his bow and blasted three monkeys into eternity. Smashing the glass case, he scooped up the missile, and then, clearly outnumbered as he was, fired back, blasting off a chunk of Lakshman's armor, before escaping through the vast cavern with the weapon.

"Lakshman!" Vibhishan called. "The Ray weapon! You must stop him!"

While Lakshman and the remaining monkeys followed cautiously, Indrajit boarded his chariot and streaked into the sky with a pulsating roar, firing arrows at Lakshman as he left the temple. Vibhishan and Hanuman, by ducking and dodging, gave Lakshman, in the shelter of a ruined wall, an opportunity to return fire, managing to punch a hole in the side of Indrajit's chariot.

When Indrajit returned fire, demolishing the wall, Lakshman ran for the shelter behind a rock. Covered by Vibhishan, Lakshman fired again, this time connecting flesh, but Indrajit battled on, hurt and bloody. Lakshman fired at Indrajit again, piercing his armor, knocking him off his seat.

Both warriors were excellent archers, and continued fighting valiantly, their straining bowstrings reaching maximum, sharp arrows scorching through the air with deadly accuracy, exploding in brilliance, hurling thunderbolts that ripped up the ground, devastating forest and pastureland. But, Indrajit fought on with a ferocity that caused Lakshman to wonder if he could ever be defeated.

Finally, Lakshman launched an intense attack, and rocked Indrajit's chariot, almost throwing him overboard, forcing him to drop the Ray weapon. As he struggled to retrieve it, Lakshman fired another volley, causing Indrajit to roll dangerously. In desperation, he began punching buttons on the console.

"He's trying to go invisible," shouted Vibhishan. "Keep him busy!"

Lakshman fired, but the demon had already vanished, and then re-appeared in another part of the sky. When Lakshman once more prepared to fire, he had an idea.

"Hanuman, take me up quick!" he shouted.

As Hanuman chanted a mantra, Lakshman jumped onto his expanding hand until soon he was at the same height as Indrajit. Buffeted by a strong wind, he loaded an astra just as Indrajit fired, momentarily blinding him. Taking advantage of Lakshman's predicament, Indrajit left the console, picked up the Ray weapon, and punched in the arming code. Swinging it onto his shoulder, he took aim at Lakshman, who, through streaming eyes, saw Indrajit prepare to fire. As Lakshman reached for another astra, he slipped on Hanuman's giant palm, spilling arrows from his quiver to the ground far below, except for one which dangled precariously from the strap, which he loaded onto his bow.

Wiping his eyes, Lakshman chanted the sacred mantra and strained back his bow till it was bent almost double, as Indrajit got him in his sights.

Lakshman's weapon screamed through the air at Indrajit, parting his head from his body.

The ray gun, and Indrajit's head, both fell to the floor of the chariot with a dull thud.

At that, a great shout went up from the Vanara army, a mighty sound heard all over the battlefield.

Immediately Ram ordered an attack. Easily overcoming the fleeing rakshas, the monkey army flooded through the city gates, destroying crossroads, platforms, and capturing assembly houses, palace frontages, granaries, treasuries, and all Ravan's flags.

A battle worn officer burst into Ravan's throne room with the news that the monkey army had broken through, and that Indrajit had been killed by Lakshman.

Queen Mandodari screamed. Ravan stood rigid, his face expressionless.

"My son, dead?"

His wife buried her face in her dress, sobbing hysterically.

"He did not complete the sacrifice for immortality, sire." The officer continued.

After a minute, Ravan recovered, his voice horribly distorted. "They will pay dearly for this! Guards, prepare my aerial chariot! And bring the real Sita! I shall not be defeated."

Shurpanak entered the room and shuffled close to the demon king.

"You seem to be losing the war, brother. Is Sita really worth all this trouble?"

"To possess the most beautiful woman in the three worlds, I will fight the entire Universe!"

As Sita was brought before him, flanked by two ugly rakshas guards, her hair unkempt; her eyes red and puffed, but her beauty still apparent, Ravan drew his sword, shuddered with anger, and stared into her eyes.

"Do you know what you have done?" he demanded. "Because of you, two of my sons, my brother, and half my army are dead. Indrajit may have killed a false Sita. But now, I shall kill the real one! You are going to die."

With his sword raised, Ravan lunged at her.

"Nooooooo!" screamed Sita, struggling against her guards, as Minister Suparswa stepped in front of her.

"Ravan, stop! You cannot do this," he implored. "Killing a woman goes against all scripture. Better to defeat Ram in battle, then you can rightfully claim Sita as your own. Today is the new moon day, the best time. Fight, and you will be successful."

Ravan shuddered again in disgust, before slowly lowering his sword. "You had better be right, Suparswa. Take her to the dungeons!" he ordered the guards. "And if by some quirk of fate, I do not survive. Kill her!"

"You will never defeat Ram," Sita cried as she was dragged away. "He is invincible! Invincible!"

"I'll kill every last one of them!" Ravan snarled, gazing out the window.

CHAPTER 45

RAVAN MEETS HIS MATCH

OUT ON THE BATTLEFIELD, the monkeys were celebrating the demise of Indrajit when Ravan appeared, standing on his chariot, his protective armor gleaming, his Generals, Chiefs of Staff, Commanders, Masters-at-Arms and soldiers, arranged around him.

"Remember Kumbakarn and Indrajit," he shouted to his troops. "Remember Aksa, Dhrumraksa, Vajradamshtra, Akampan and Prahastha. Remember all our brave warriors. Spare no one. Kill them all."

The rakshas army cheered.

"And if anyone tries to leave the battlefield," he continued, "I will personally cut out his heart!"

Ravan signaled the attack, and the rakshas armies spewed onto the battlefield like a tidal wave as rockets exploded around the grieving Ram mobilizing his troops to the west. Advancing rapidly, the hordes of rakshas clashed with the monkeys, both sides reeking havoc, the air full of the odor of scorching missiles and the screams of dying warriors.

A frightful roar filled the air and Ravan's black war chariot, surrounded by a purple phosphorescent halo, and pulled by goblin-headed mules, thundered across the sky.

Blood rained down onto the chariot, and violent whirlwinds blew from left to right as a flock of vultures followed the demon king. Huge meteors fell, accompanied by deep rumbling thunder. She-jackals and vultures howled as the sky turned black and the earth quaked.

Then the fighting stopped, while all on the battlefield stood motionless, watching the incensed Ravan circle the battlefield, rubbing his left eye.

To even the odds, Indra, ruler of the gods, decreed that Ram would also have a chariot, and a golden car appeared, pulled by six white horses with white colored whisks decorated with golden ornaments on their heads, and garlanded with nets of gold. Hundreds of small golden bells tinkled on its roof, precious stones shimmered on its pillars, and a gem-covered pole, from which fluttered a standard, shone brilliantly.

Ram mounted the car, knowing the time had come for the devil that stole his wife, but did not battle with a hateful heart; that would not be fitting for such a pious prince. To give a suffering person like Ravan, relief from the miseries of material life, was better. Ravan was the embodiment of all that was evil, and the price for his actions was high. But, to be killed by the eighth incarnation of Vishnu, the Supreme Personality of Godhead, meant liberation from the material world.

Ram took off, accelerating up to Ravan's altitude, and closed on the demon king.

Out on the battlefield, only the breeze stirred, curling up the dust and fluttering the tattered pennants. All else was silent as Ram soared upward and turned his chariot to face Ravan. As he did so, the sky filled with Devas, Danavas, *Apsaras*, *Kinnaras*, Gandharvas, *Maharishis* and demigods, the good souls of the Universe.

"The time has come for you to pay for your sins," Ram said resolutely. "You abducted my wife Sita. You are no better than a dog who steals from the kitchen of his absent master."

With that, Ram kicked his chariot into a shallow dive, and the team of white horses sped through the air towards Ravan, who fired an astra at Ram that rattled his chariot and seared his face with its heat as it rocketed past. Thunder tore at Ram's ears, momentarily deafening him. Another second and he would have been burnt to a cinder. His chariot shook violently and lost height, but he managed to recover and bring it under control. The shock of the near miss pushed him to a higher level of awareness, and he became calm, filled with purpose and resolve.

Turning again, he headed for Ravan with a vengeance, unleashing an astra as he flew past. To his amazement, although Ravan's chariot exploded, he managed to fly it.

Ravan targeted Ram again, this time sending a *shoola* trident weapon thundering towards him, its three separate warheads hurling themselves straight at the Prince, only to see them shot down by Ram's *shakti* arrows. In return, Ravan fired an *agni* weapon, its fire lighting up the entire sky. Ram counterattacked with a water weapon, dowsing the flames. When Ravan fired another astra, blowing a corner off Ram's chariot, Ram quickly checked the damage.

"Enough, Ravan," he called. "Your time has come."

Turned tightly, Ram commenced another run. Weaving and dodging, he closed on Ravan, judging the angle and distance, waiting till he was absolutely sure of a hit.

A few seconds later, he had him in his sights.

"Say your prayers, demon!" yelled Ram, as he stretched back the bowstring, bow glowing green. Ravan couldn't avoid the ball of fire as it whistled towards him, and the arrow shot straight and true, blasting his head from his body.

"Ravan is finished!" yelled a jubilant Lakshman. "No one could have survived that!"

Ravan's torso crumpled to the floor of his chariot as the demon army stood wide-eyed and devastated.

As for the Vanaras, they shouted and danced triumphantly, waving their arms and chanting, "Ram, Ram, Ram, Prince Ram, Ram, Ram!"

Vibhishan did not share their enthusiasm, however.

"Don't underestimate the power of Ravan," he warned Lakshman, his eyes locked on the listing chariot. "His mystical potency extends far beyond our level of understanding. A dark, demonic nature flows through him like a river, deep and uninviting, full of evil. His defeat will not come about so easily."

"What do you mean?" Lakshman demanded, "Ravan is dead; Ram killed him. I saw it myself!"

And indeed, Ravan's chariot still hovered in position, listing at a crazy angle, his torso lying like a bloated whale, oozing blood. Suddenly, Ravan's foot twitched! A hand shook! Ravan's torso moved! The headless body began to shake and convulse! The monkeys cheering faltered. Ravan sat up! Then stood up! Their hopes dashed, the monkeys ran for cover. Ram stared in disbelief as he saw Ravan come back to life.

"What is that?" he said incredulously.

Then, Ravan's frame shook, and a new head appeared on his shoulders. Ravan shook again, and another head appeared, and then another! Within seconds ten heads had grown on his shoulders, all the mouths spitting fire, every eye blazing like an erupting volcano. From his side twenty black arms appeared, each holding mystical weapons.

He disappeared, creating in his absence, goblins and ghouls with bows and arrows; and yoginis, holding swords in one hand, skulls in the other, from which they drank blood.

When Ravan appeared again, Ram lost no time. He fired at the demon, severing one of the heads, and the sky darkened, casting an eerie light over the battlefield. Animals howled and the wind screamed, thunder rumbled, lightning flashed, and comets streamed across the heavens.

Then Ravan grew another head.

Undeterred, Ram continued to load and fire at Ravan's heads, but they kept growing. "Fool," they cried in unison. "You can't kill me! I am the greatest warrior! Prepare to die!"

"What do I do?" cried Ram, as he brought his chariot round. "Is there no way to stop this madness?"

Then a familiar voice entered his consciousness.

"The Brahmastra weapon. Use it only to uphold the highest ideal."

"Agastya!"

Remembering his training, Ram pulled out the Crescent Moon arrow from its special place in the quiver.

"It cannot be recalled," the voice reminded him, "Choose your target well."

Ram was in the moment. He knew the balance of power lay in his hands, and that the three realms looked to him for liberation.

Covered in perspiration, concentration etched in his face, Ram loaded the astra, bending the bow to breaking point. Taking careful aim, he softly chanted the mystic mantra taught by Agastya, and the tingling bow glowed like burnished gold as he focused on the dark form of Ravan, writhing in his rocking chariot. For a second he held it, then released.

The Crescent Moon arrow leapt across the sky with a high-pitched whine and buried itself in Ravan's chest. The demon's hysterical laughter changed to a hideous scream as the Brahmastra exploded in a brilliant strobe of light. The deathly breath of Brahma's fire had, at last, broken the black heart of the mortal pretender.

The blast of hot air that followed raced across the battlefield and caused Ram's chariot to pitch and roll, showering debris everywhere. Those not holding onto something were flung around like scraps of paper on a blustery day.

After the dust had cleared, a hypnotic silence descended all around.

The war was over.

CHAPTER 46

A NEW BEGINNING

THE SILENCE WAS SHATTERED by the sound of trumpets, and the arrival of hundreds of women, led by Queen Mandodari. Looking up at the sky in anguish and calling Ravan's name, they fell to the ground, crying in grief.

Then a strange thing happened. The battlefield suddenly transformed into a lovely meadow, with colorful flowers and blossoming trees appearing everywhere. Birds sang and crickets clicked. Rakshas converged from all parts of the erstwhile battlefield, hands held high in surrender, along with monkey soldiers, released prisoners from the city's prisons, and townspeople.

Queen Mandodari was overcome with grief. "Forgive us all," she sobbed. "May Sita be reunited with her husband the most merciful Ram, without delay."

As everyone converged on the blackened, ruined palace, Ram sprinted across the courtyard closely followed by Lakshman, past great heaps of shattered masonry, where thunderbolts had struck with such devastating force, Sita, the only thing on his mind. "Was she alive? Had Ravan's renegade soldiers harmed her?"

"Sita! Sita!" he called frantically.

In an instant, Ram was up the stairway, ready to blast his way into the palace, but stopped dead in his tracks as the huge door slowly creaked open, revealing Hanuman, close to tears.

Ram just stared, his heart pounding wildly. "Was this the end? Was Sita dead?"

Then the door fully opened, and right in front of him, escorted by two maidens, was Sita, dressed in a golden sari and red robe, jewels and flower ornaments adorning her black hair, looking exactly like the Sita at the cottage so long ago, before the arrival of Ravan.

She gazed at Ram, eyes full of tears, and in two steps was in his arms.

The monkeys, seeing Sita for the first time, gathered at the bottom of the stairway, staring madly.

"So this is the Princess we were fighting for," said one of them.

"She is so beautiful," said another.

Ram took Sita's delicate head in his hands, wiped away her tears, and looked deeply into her beautiful lotus eyes.

"Oh, my Sita," he murmured low.

"My Lord," Sita whispered in return.

The monkeys giggled as Hanuman turned away to hide his emotions. Then Ram and Sita descended the staircase, staring across the battlefield at the thousands of bodies lying on the ground.

"Oh, Lord Indra, now the battle is won," Ram said, raising his eyes to the heavens, "please bring back to life all those brave warriors who died to save my Sita."

A sweet scent permeated the air, and millions of flower petals, marigold, rose, sweet pea, lilac, and honeysuckle, every color of the rainbow, fell like snow about them. Whereupon, the dead monkeys and bears started to move, and came back to life. Getting slowly to their feet, they brushed the petals off, and offered prayers to the heavens.

The crowd broke into a chant, "Glories to Prince Ram, Glories to Prince Ram!"

Outside the burnt out ruins of Ravan's palace, townsfolk perched on the top of every wall and ledge to watch as Vibhishan, accompanied by four servants, removed his helmet, bowed, and dropped on one knee before Ram. Picking up his sword, Ram lightly touched him on the shoulder and said, "Vibhishan, I appoint you new King of Lanka. May you rule perfectly, in peace and prosperity."

After asking Vibhishan to preside over the funeral ceremonies of Ravan and those members of his family who were killed, Ram went on to address the people of Lanka.

"Ravan's reign of tyranny is over," he declared. "From now on, Lanka will be a city free of evil and vice, a city with a new king, a new way of life, and new hope."

The crowd cheered. Kettledrums pounded. Tom-toms thundered. And a celestial vision of King Dasarath appeared in the sky.

"You have done well, my son," boomed Dasarath from the heavens. "By your actions, you have proven that good can prevail over evil. I am proud of you, Ram. Lakshman, you have served Ram well, may you receive just merit in Vaikuntha."

As Dasarath disappeared, the heavens lit up and the gods sounded their trumpets in celebration, while below, the crowds chanted Ram's name again and again, "Glories to Prince Ram! Glories to Prince Ram!"

And there were more marvels to behold. Sitting in their ships, high above the trees, appeared Lord Kubera, Lord Yama, Indra, Varuna, Siva, Brahma, and all the Celestials, followed by the *Puspaka* flower chariot of Lord Vishnu, pulled by a huge white swan.

Garuda, the swan carrier, floated through the air, and touched down smoothly in the courtyard, barely ruffling a feather.

"Vibhishan, I am most grateful for all that you have done," Ram said, turning to his friend. "You will always have my blessing and protection. May you rule over the new Lanka in peace."

"Thank you, Prince Ram," Vibhishan responded. "I shall never forget you."

"Go in peace," Ram said, embracing him, "and build a prosperous kingdom."

And boarding Garuda through a shower of flower petals, Ram and Sita waved as the giant craft slowly rose into the sky, and disappeared in the direction of Ayodhya.

CHAPTER 47

RETURN TO AYODHYA

IN NANDIGRAM, BHARAT, HAVING seen a fleet of golden vimana aircraft approaching, arranged in a circle around a puspaka chariot, understood Ram was returning, and ordered celebrations to begin in Ayodhya. As a result, Ram, Sita and Lakshman arrived over Ayodhya to a fantastic pyrotechnic display launched from the city walls as the citizens spilled out into the streets and cheered wildly.

Once landed, they made their way up the wide steps to the Royal palace of Ayodhya, to where an exquisitely decorated throne sat on a raised dais surrounded by thousands of happy citizens. Ram and Sita walked along the red carpet while children threw flowers at their feet, to join Kausalya, Sumitra, and Kaikeyi standing with Srutakirti on one side of the throne, with Visvamitra, the Rishis, and Shatrughna, holding Ram's bow and quivers. On the other side stood Janaka and his wife, Agastya, Hanuman, carrying an umbrella,

Vibhishan, holding a whisk, Sugriva, holding a fan, Angada, carrying a sword, and Jambavan, carrying a golden shield. When Urmila saw Lakshman, she ran to him and threw herself into his arms.

Bharat and Mandavi greeted the Royal Couple as they walked towards the throne, Sita carrying a pot containing water from all the holy places.

"Welcome home, brother," said Bharat, "the throne awaits you, and so do your people."

"Thank you, Bharat," Ram said as they embraced one another. "It's good to be back in Ayodhya."

After Bharat had removed Ram's slippers from the base of the throne, and placed them on his elder brother's feet, Ram sat down, and sank slowly into the same luxurious red cushion his father had sat on all those years ago, while a purple cloak was draped around his shoulders, and a golden crown, studded with precious stones, gently placed on his head.

Sita sat beside him as Vasishtha sprinkled them with sanctified water.

Prompted by Lord Indra, Vayu, the god of the wind, placed a garland of one hundred golden lotuses around Ram's shoulders, and gifted Sita with a handsome necklace made of pearls.

Ram and Sita looked at each other with deep love and affection as gifts were laid at their feet. Trumpets sounded, kettledrums played, heavenly choirs sang, and the people of Ayodhya danced in the streets.

Then Sita looked anxiously around, and took off her necklace.

"Give it to the one who deserves it most," said Ram, reading her thoughts.

Sita went to Sugriva's general, and placed the pearls around his neck.

"Thank you, Hanuman," she said gratefully, as the crowd broke into thunderous applause.

THE END

Today, the Festival of *Diwali*, marking the return of Sita and Ram to Ayodhya, is celebrated in October all over the world, and Ayodhya also attracts its share of pilgrims for the Festival of Lights, re-enacting that triumphal return.

As long as the mountains and rivers flourish on the surface of the earth, the Ramayan story will be told, and persons who read and repeat this divine epic will be liberated from all sinful reactions and promoted to the spiritual abode.

AUTHOR BIO

HE STUDIED THE *VEDIC* literature for twenty-two years, which included *Ramayan*, *Mahabharata* and *Bhagavad-gita*, and traveled to India, visiting many holy sites, participating in numerous spiritual festivals.

He presently lives on the West Coast of the USA.

Ramayan book website: www.ramayanbook.com

GLOSSARY

Agastya	a powerful rishi in the forest
Agni	the Lord of Fire
Akampan	a general of Ravan
Aksa	son of Ravan
Angada	a monkey Prince
Apsaras	celestial nymphs
Artharva Veda	the fourth Veda
Ashram	a religious community
Ashvamedha	sacrificial ceremony
Ashvapati	the father of Kaikeyi, King of Keykaya
Ashoka	a minister of Dasarath
Astra	a missile
Asuras	demoniac beings
Ayodhya	the birthplace of Lord Ram
Bharadvaja	a holy man in the Dandaka forest
Bharat	the brother of Lord Ram
Brahma	the first created living being
Danavas	demoniac beings
Dandaka	a large forest near Ayodhya

Dasarath	King of Kosala, father of Lord Ram
Devas	godly beings
Dharma	religious duty
Dhriti	a minister of Dasarath
Dhumraksa	a general of Ravan
Diwali	the festival celebrating Ram's return to Ayodhya
Dushana	the brother of Ravan
Garuda	the carrier of Lord Vishnu
Gandharvas	celestial singers
Gurudeva	a guru or holy man
Hanuman	a minister of Sugriva and devotee of Lord Ram
Haradhanu	the bow of Siva
Indra	King of the heavenly planets
Indrajit	the son of Ravan
Ishvakus	family line of Lord Ram
Jabali	a counselor of Ayodhya
Jambavan	the chief of bears in Sugriva's army
Janaka	King of Mithila
Jatayu	a divine eagle
Jayanta	a minister of Dasarath
Kaikeyi	the mother of Bharat
Karma	the law of reaction to action
Kashyapa	a counselor of Ayodhya
Kausalya	mother of Lord Ram
Keykeya	country to the north west of Kosala
Khara	the brother of Ravan
Kinnaras	an ancient tribe of celestial beings
Kishkinda	the city of monkeys
Kosala	a country under the rule of Dasarath

Ksatriya	the warrior class
Kumba	son of Kumbakarn
Kumbakarn	the giant brother of Ravan
Lakshman	the brother of Lord Ram
Lankini	protecting goddess of Lanka
Mahaparshva	a general of Ravan
Maharishi	a rishi who has performed great austerities
Mahodara	a general of Ravan
Malyavan	the grandfather of Ravan
Mandavi	the wife of Bharat
Mandodari	the wife of Ravan
Manthara	a maidservant of Kaikeyi
Mantras	sound vibrations or incantations
Marichi	the wizard and uncle of Ravan
Markendeya	a counselor of Ayodhya
Maya	illusion
Mithila	kingdom of Janaka
Nagapasa	the serpent missile
Nala	monkey engineer who built a bridge to Lanka
Nandigram	where Bharat lived while Ram was in exile
Narayan	the fourhanded expansion of Lord Krishna
Neela	a monkey General
Nikumba	the son of Kumbakarn
Nikumbila	place where Indrajit prayed for immortality
Panchavati	place where Lord Rama built a cottage
Prahastha	the Commander-in-Chief of Ravan's army
Puspaka	flower chariot
Rakshas	a demon
Ram	an incarnation of the Supreme Lord

Ravan	the demon King of Lanka
Rishi	a holy man
Rishyasringa	a priest of Ayodhya
Sampati	the brother of Jatayu
Samudra	Lord of the Ocean
Sanskrit	the language of the Vedas
Sarayu	tributary of the Ganges
Satananda	a family priest of King Janak
Shakti	a missile
Shatrughna	the brother of Lord Ram
Shoola	a multi-headed missile
Shurpanak	half-sister of Ravan
Siddhartha	a minister of Dasarath
Sita	the wife of Lord Ram, daughter of King Janak
Sudaman	King Janak's chief councilor
Sugriva	the monkey King
Sumantra	a minister of Dasarath
Sumitra	Queen of Dasarath, mother of Lakshman
Suyagnya	a counselor of Ayodhya
Srutakirti	wife of Shatrughna
Sunayana	wife of King Janak
Suparswa	the son of Sampati
Sushena	a monkey physician
Tapasya	austerities
Trijata	head demoness in Lanka
Urmila	the wife of Lakshman
Vajradamshtra	a general of Ravan
Vamadeva	the family priest of Ayodhya
Varana	a monkey

Vasishtha	the guru of Ayodhya
Vayu	the god of the wind, father of Hanuman
Vibhishan	the brother of Ravan
Vijaya	a minister of Dasarath
Vimana	spacecraft
Virupaksha	a general of Ravan
Vishnu	the Supreme Personality of Godhead
Visvakarma	the celestial architect
Yajna	a sacrificial ceremony
Yaksas	attendants to Kubera, the god of wealth
Visvamitra	a great sage
Yojana	a distance of about nine miles
Yuhajit	the brother of Kaikeyi

CPSIA information can be obtained
at www.ICGtesting.com
Printed in the USA
LVHW041549291022
731887LV00006B/174

9 780595 507634